AGAINST ALL ODDS

STACY CLAFLIN

AGAINST ALL ODDS
AN ALEX MERCER THRILLER #4
by Stacy Claflin
http://www.stacyclaflin.com

Receive free books from the author:
http://stacyclaflin.com/newsletter

To all the victims of school shootings

I finished this manuscript the morning of the Stoneman Douglas massacre. I struggled with whether to change it or even to not release it, but these tragedies are something we face as a society. Exploring these issues through story is part of how I process difficult events and situations. I hope reading this novel helps you work through your feelings, too.

CONTENTS

1. Attack — 1
2. Terror — 5
3. Frantic — 9
4. Mess — 13
5. Trapped — 18
6. Pursuit — 21
7. Bomb — 27
8. Detained — 31
9. Corral — 35
10. Tied — 39
11. Finally — 45
12. Contrast — 50
13. Fretting — 55
14. Room — 59
15. Overwhelm — 62
16. Connection — 67
17. Relief — 71
18. Struggle — 75
19. Sweet — 78
20. Mistake — 82
21. Emergency — 86
22. Fight — 91
23. Time — 95
24. Conflicted — 99
25. Shock — 103
26. Convince — 107
27. Question — 111
28. Intimidation — 116
29. Intimidation — 120
30. Search — 124
31. Epiphany — 128
32. Truth — 134

33. Lead 140
34. Flee 147
35. Guilt 152
36. Nowhere 154
37. Surprise 159
38. Temptation 165
39. Crushed 168
40. Back 172
41. Convince 175
42. Cabin 180
43. Horrified 184
44. Explain 190
45. Alone 194
46. Despair 197
47. Confusion 200
48. Regret 204
49. Hidden 209
50. Assault 214
51. Pursue 219
52. Racing 224
53. Held 230
54. Chase 236
55. Hospital 240
56. Resting 244
57. Over 249
58. Secrets 254

Author's Note 259
No Return 261
When Tomorrow Starts Without Me 265
Story Worlds by Stacy Claflin 271
Other Books 273

ATTACK

Ava Fleshman leaned over the sink and studied her makeup in the mirror. She'd done a decent job of covering the dark circles under her eyes. Not that she cared what anyone thought.

She pulled out a tube of the darkest red lipstick she'd been able to find, and swiped it carefully across her lower lip. Halfway through her top lip, she froze.

Screaming sounded outside the middle school bathroom.

Probably just a group of kids skipping class, like her.

Ava finished her lipstick, then turned around.

The shouts grew louder. Frantic.

Footsteps thundered, sounding like a stampede.

Someone yelled the word *gun*.

Her heart skipped a beat, then raced. The lipstick fell from her grasp and bounced on the tile floor.

Ava couldn't move. Did someone really have a gun? As in, a real one? Not just some stupid prank, like Connor Johnson pulled last year?

She crept to the door and pulled it open a crack. Just enough to peek out with one eye.

Kids ran in all directions, some yelling and others crying. Bags, books, and other items lay strewn about.

Boom!

It sounded like a firecracker echoing down the hallway.

Ava knew better. It was a gunshot.

No, this was nothing like what Connor had pulled a year earlier.

Someone ran toward the bathroom. He pushed on the door before Ava had a chance to move. The door hit her in the nose. Hard.

Blood gushed out and her nose throbbed.

"Watch it!" She shoved the football player and covered her nose.

"Hide!" Ryker pushed past her and jumped into one of the stalls.

Ava dropped her bag and ran into another stall, still covering her nose. Blood now dripped down from her palm onto her white shirt. She grabbed a bunch of toilet paper and held it up to her nostrils as she climbed on top of the seat.

The bathroom door opened and shut several times. Two girls cried.

"Shut up!" Ava demanded. "You want the shooter to come in here and find us?"

Bang!

Another gunshot. It was even closer than the first one.

The crying girls both screamed.

Those idiots were going to not only get themselves killed, but everyone else in the bathroom—including Ava.

Rage ran through her. She dropped the red wad of toilet paper into the water and marched out of the stall.

The two screamers were clinging to each other, makeup smeared all the way down both of their faces.

Ava clenched her fists and glared at them. "You have a death wish?"

Still sobbing, they both shook their heads.

"Then shut up! I don't want to die today, either."

They quieted, other than breathing heavily.

It was all Ava could hear.

Everything else was calm.

Too calm.

Terror squeezed every inch of her. Ava's pulse drummed in her ears as she creeped toward the door. Her hand seemed to act on its own as she reached for the handle.

One of the girls behind her let out another cry.

Ava spun around and glowered at her. "Get ahold of yourself!"

She shut her mouth and buried her face against her friend's shoulder.

Ava turned back around and pulled the door open slightly. Other than the abandoned items, the hall was empty.

"Is he out there?" whispered one of the criers.

Ava shook her head and opened the door a little wider. Everything was still silent. Even the two girls who were huddled behind her.

She pulled on the door until she was able to fit her head through.

Footsteps sounded from the hallway. One heavy, plodding step after the next. They echoed in the empty corridor.

Ava turned toward the noise.

The man wore all black leathers and brandished a rifle. He also had two pistols attached to his belt.

He hadn't seen her yet. Ava needed to step back into the bathroom. But something stopped her.

She knew the man.

His gaze locked on hers. "Ava."

Her blood went cold.

"I've been looking for you."

She swallowed. "Get away from me!"

He laughed, then aimed his weapon at her.

Ava ducked back in and pushed on the door. "Someone help me!"

The two girls scurried into a stall.

"Help, Ryker!" Ava cried.

The gunman pushed on the door.

Ryker ran out from the stall and shoved his shoulder against the door.

Ava had never been happier to see a linebacker in her life. But even with the two of them pushing on the door, it still moved in toward them.

"Ava, give up before your friends die!" shouted the gunman.

Ryker turned to her, wide-eyed. "You know him?"

Her stomach twisted in knots. She couldn't bring herself to admit the truth.

"Give yourself up, and nobody else has to die!"

Ryker continued staring at her, his face paling. "Is he really going to kill us if you don't go out there?"

Ava's stomach lurched. Her nose throbbed. The bathroom spun around her.

"Ava…" Something tapped the door. It was probably the rifle.

Ryker stepped back. "Sorry." He fled back to his stall.

The door burst open. Ava stumbled back. She tripped over her bag and clung to a sink to keep from falling.

Her mother's ex-boyfriend entered the bathroom and knitted his brows together.

Ava's knees shook as she stared at the gunman. "Wh-what are you d-doing here, Dave?"

His nostrils flared. "You won't be the one asking questions."

"Does this have to do with my mom?"

Dave stepped toward her and shoved the gun against her chest. Ava screamed.

TERROR

Captain Nick Fleshman slunk into his chair and rubbed his temples. He usually stayed out of the interrogation room, but the suspect had worn down his best guys. And now he'd worn out Nick, too. All he wanted to do was to go back home and climb into bed for a few hours. Or maybe he could at least take a long lunch.

Instead, all hell broke loose outside his office. People shouted and ran around in all directions.

Nick flew to his feet and flung his door open. "What's going on?"

Foster turned to him, stopping in her tracks. Her face was noticeably pale. "There's a gunman at the middle school."

"What?" He leaned against the doorway, unable to breathe. It had to be a joke. Two of his three kids were at the middle school.

"There have been shots. It's all hands on deck. Other precincts are coming in with us."

Nick shook his head and took a deep breath. "Meet me at your cruiser."

She nodded, then ran down the hallway, darting between other officers.

Nick ran around his office, grabbing everything he needed for an incident of this caliber. His mind raced. His hands shook.

Thank God he was on the force and could go inside the building. He couldn't imagine being one of the parents forced to wait outside behind a yellow line.

Were Parker and Ava safe? Had everything he'd ever taught them stuck with them? They'd always thought he was crazy for drilling them on how to respond in an emergency, but he knew all too well the dangers of the world, even living in a fairly small community.

Nick hurried outside. Police cruisers were already fleeing the parking lot, sirens blazing. Foster pulled out of the parking spot before Nick had even closed his door.

"We'll do everything we can," she assured him.

Nick snapped his seatbelt into place. "Is Tinsley at school today?"

"No." Foster turned on the lights and siren, then pulled onto the road. "She's in therapy all morning."

"At least that's one less kid to worry about."

"I can't imagine what more trauma would do to her. She's barely making progress as it is."

"Right, sorry. I wasn't thinking about that."

The girl had been saved after a shootout—her mother had been a dangerous kidnapper and her father a criminal, now both dead. Tinsley would only talk to Officer Foster, and afterward she'd been kind enough to take the girl in and work with her.

"No, it's okay." Foster honked at a station wagon that didn't get out of their way fast enough, then went around into the other lane. "There's a lot going on, and your kids..." Her voice trailed off.

"Yeah." Nick took a deep breath. "I just hope no kids were hurt. None of them deserves to deal with this."

The school came into view, and it was a mess. Fire trucks, ambulances, and police were there. Frantic parents swarmed the area, not that Nick could blame them. But it was going to make it all that much harder to process the scene—which would be a nightmare without all the added people.

He radioed in that they were there. The only update they received was that the shooter was still on the loose. No ID on the suspect. It could be anyone.

He and Foster exchanged a glance before bursting out of the car and racing over to the scene. They weaved between crying and worried parents until they reached the yellow tape and went under it.

From where Nick stood, the middle school looked normal. Almost like it should on a regular school day. Except for the flashing lights from the emergency vehicles.

They both drew their weapons, then Nick reached for the door.

Inside was a completely different scene. Abandoned backpacks strewn across the hall. Several lockers wide open. Even a shoe lay in the corner by itself.

Nick shuddered. Where were all the kids? Where were *his* kids?

A deputy and a detective ran down the hall, all but ignoring Nick and Foster.

"Hey!" Nick called.

The deputy turned to them. "Just got word about bodies in the office. All adults." He and the detective raced down the hallway.

Nick's stomach tightened. He and Foster followed. Now that Nick's two oldest kids were back in town and attending the school, he knew the way to the office without needing to follow anyone.

The first thing he saw was the blood spatter on the windows.

On the radio, he heard news of kids hiding in the cafeteria.

Nick turned to Foster. "Let's go."

Without a word, they spun around and raced in the other direction. They ran into other first responders heading there.

"Where are all the kids?" Nick demanded.

"We've directed them to the back to be checked out by the medics. Officers are there to get their statements."

"Still no suspect?"

He shook his head.

"Kid? Adult? Does anyone know?"

"Not yet, but with all the kids we're processing, it shouldn't be long."

They rounded a corner. Wailing sounded from the cafeteria.

Nick prepared himself for the worst.

What he saw was just a roomful of terrorized kids. No blood, no physical injuries. No gunman.

They split up and helped the kids into the hallway, toward the medics outside. Neither Parker nor Ava were in there. He couldn't see them outside with the medics, either.

He and Foster headed inside to search the rest of the building. It could take all day with so many classrooms, closets, and other places to hide.

His cell phone hadn't stopped going off in his pocket. Everyone he knew probably wanted to know if their kids were safe. He had the same question about his own children, and being police captain didn't bring him answers any faster than it did the regular citizens. It just meant he didn't have to stand outside looking in.

The radio went off—it hadn't stopped—but this time it was different.

A bomb threat had been called in.

The caller claimed to be the shooter, and that he had a hostage.

Nick turned to Foster. "I'm going to keep looking for kids. They're probably hiding everywhere, scared out of their minds."

She nodded. "I'm not leaving until everyone living is outside."

"Let's comb through this place, but don't believe for a moment that the gunman actually left."

FRANTIC

Alex Mercer stared at the news on his phone. Someone was firing a gun at the middle school?

His bedroom spun around him, and he clenched the blankets with his free hand while scrolling for more information.

But there was nothing. A shooter at Ariana's school.

Hadn't their family been through enough? Ariana had, and she was only twelve. She had already survived an abduction with a madman a year and a half before.

Alex scrambled out of bed, throwing on clothes without paying attention to what he grabbed. Dirty, mismatched—he didn't care.

He called Zoey as he pulled on some questionable socks, but instead of ringing, it went to voicemail.

Next, he called Nick. His friend the police captain would know what was going on. That went to voicemail, too. He was probably in the thick of it.

Alex put on a Mariner's cap and made a few more calls as he made his way out the door of his apartment.

It seemed the whole town was ignoring their phones.

On his way to his new-to-him little sedan, he called his future in-laws. The legal parents of his daughter who he'd given up for adoption when he was just fourteen.

Valerie answered. "H-hi, Alex." The tougher-than-nails woman was crying.

He leaned against his car, horrible images filling his mind. "Where's Ariana?"

"Sick in bed." Valerie sniffled. "She woke up with flu symptoms this morning."

Alex took a deep breath. "Thank God." He'd never been happier to hear about anyone having the flu.

Valerie continued sobbing on the other end.

Alex readjusted his baseball cap. "What's the matter?"

"Zoey."

He bolted upright. "What about her?"

Valerie sniffled again. "Zoey went to the school to pick up homework for Ariana. Nobody can reach her."

The words felt like a punch to the gut. Alex fell back against his car, struggling to breathe. His fiancée was at the school? The woman he'd loved since he was Ariana's age? Zoey was the love of his life, and they were finally engaged. They had picked a date and were in the process of choosing a venue.

He struggled to find his voice. "Zoey's there?"

"We don't know that she actually made it. But nobody can reach her. Can you try?"

A lump in his throat choked him. "I already did."

Valerie sobbed again.

"Alex?" Kenji's unstable voice came through the phone.

"Yeah." Alex hoped his soon-to-be father-in-law would tell him Valerie was mistaken.

He didn't. "If you hear anything from Nick, call us right away."

Alex's vision grew blurry. "Yeah, of course. I can't reach him either."

"I'm sure he's busy." Kenji cleared his throat. "I need to check on Ari."

"You're not going to tell her about any of this, are you?"

"Not a chance, but she does have a phone and a laptop, so she might find out. We can't shelter her forever."

"Yes, we can. Ariana has the flu. She doesn't need either of those things. The last thing she needs is to know about the shooting or her mom possibly being there."

"I know, I know."

"Then take those devices out of her room! Or I'll come over there myself."

"Right now, she's so feverish she doesn't want to get out of bed. I don't think she'll be interested in her phone today."

Alex swore. "Is she going to be okay? Should I bring something? Take her to the doctor?"

"You find our Zoey. We'll take care of Ari. Okay?"

"Yeah, sure." Alex ended the call and ran his fingers through his hair. What was he supposed to do? Go to the school and see if she was there?

It seemed like the only thing he could do. Valerie had said nobody could reach Zoey. That most likely meant they'd asked her coworkers.

He took several deep breaths and cleared his throat. It didn't help. Nothing would until he knew Zoey was okay.

Maybe there was a good reason for her not answering the phone. She might be helping injured kids.

Or her brain could be splattered across a wall.

Stop!

"Pull yourself together, Mercer." How would he ever make it as a cop if he couldn't think straight in an emergency?

He was finally due to start the academy next month, but would he be in a good state? Only if Zoey was alive and well. Otherwise, becoming a cadet would get pushed aside indefinitely.

Alex pulled out his phone to call his dad. His thumb hovered over the call button, but he ended up turning off the screen. With his family's luck, either Macy or his parents were also at the school for some random reason.

It wasn't out of the question. Macy had clients that attended the middle school, and she'd visited them there before. Her parents had also gone there to share with classes about their careers. It would be the Mercer luck that all three of them had been there at the same time as the shooter.

The miracle was that Ariana had been spared.

If any of his family was also there, he didn't want to know. At least not yet.

He needed to get to the school. Once there, he could hopefully figure out what he needed to know. All he needed was to see Zoey alive and well.

Alex drew in several deep breaths until he could finally see straight. Then he climbed into the car and drove like a maniac toward the middle school.

MESS

Alex had to park two blocks from the school. Given all the flashing lights, every cop in town was there. That explained how he'd avoided getting pulled over for his erratic driving.

The parking lot was filled with people. He could see that from two blocks away.

Alex ran the two blocks, terror gripping him harder with each step he took. He kept waiting for his phone to ring. But it remained silent.

There was no way he would get near the building. Aside from it being roped off, people filled the grounds like balls in a kids' ball pit. Firemen, medics, and cops wandered around, herding and helping others. Parents clung to one another, crying. A few people were reuniting with their children.

Worst of all, people were recording the chaos. Cell phones captured parents in their most excruciating moments. Some TV cameras focused on the building, while others recorded interviews. It made Alex's stomach turn. He had to look away before losing his temper.

He didn't see anyone he knew. Not Zoey, not Nick, and not

anyone else on the force. There were plenty of officers bustling around, but most of their uniforms showed they were from other towns.

It was too bad he wasn't at least a cadet. Maybe, just maybe, they would've let him on the other side of the yellow tape. They needed all the help they could get, right? But he was just a regular citizen, so it didn't matter.

He pressed his way through the crowd toward the building. If he could find a police officer he knew, they might tell him more than what they were releasing to the general public.

As Alex made his way through, he saw a parent he recognized. A friend of Ariana's. Then another and another.

Everyone was as desperate as he was. Hopefully, they would all be able to go home with their loved ones safe and sound, just shaken.

His pulse drummed in his ears, drowning out the noise of the crowd. He wanted to run but felt as though he were walking through quicksand.

At last, he reached the yellow line. Several officers stood on the other side, making sure everyone stayed on the correct side.

Alex knew one of them. He pushed his way over to him. "Detective Garcia, can you tell me anything?"

The detective stared at Alex for a moment before recognizing him. "Mercer. No, sorry. Can't say anything."

Alex pleaded with his eyes. "Nothing?"

"It's an active investigation."

"Come on. I'm a future brother in blue, not a journalist."

Garcia gave him a sympathetic glance and stepped closer, speaking quietly. "If you have a kid here, go by the ambulances. That's where they're sending everyone."

"Is anyone dead?"

"I can't comment."

Alex stared the detective down.

Garcia gave a slight nod, then turned away.

Alex spun around, muttering a string of profanities. Who was dead? How many? Was Zoey among them? Any of his other family members?

There were few things Alex hated more than feeling helpless, and with Zoey inside the building, they may as well have castrated him. If he could've gotten away with it, he'd have barged in and tried to find her. No, he would've found her, but not without getting himself arrested in the process.

All the more reason to make sure he made it to, and through, the academy.

Around back, everything was just as crazy as in front. Ambulances were parked all over the playing fields. Parents swarmed the area. Kids and teachers waited in lines for medical attention. And to give statements, no doubt.

Alex scanned the area. He saw some of Ari's friends and even her boyfriend, Scout. The kid looked like he would pass out any moment.

Still looking for Zoey, Alex made his way over to the boy. "You okay?"

He shook his head.

"Are you hurt?"

Scout tugged on his shirt. "I... I was going to the office to get something for my teacher. Then—" He shook uncontrollably, tears shining in his eyes.

Alex put his arm around Scout's shoulders. "What?"

"I heard what sounded like a firecracker. Then blood spattered on the window." He drew in a deep breath and shook harder. "It was the nurse. She died. Right there. Right in front of me."

Alex pulled him close and held him tight. He didn't know what to say. Nothing could make it better. The kid had just witnessed someone getting their brains blown out.

Scout sobbed, and Alex held him tighter. He tried to recall if he'd seen the boy's parents in the throng of people in the parking lot.

Finally, Scout pulled back. He looked up at Alex. "Do you know if Ari's okay?"

He nodded. "Home with the flu."

Scout stumbled forward, a look of relief on his face.

Alex steadied him. "Have you seen the medics yet?"

The boy shook his head.

"Let's get you over there." Alex guided him over to a paramedic who was bandaging up a girl's arm. "This boy saw what happened in the office."

The paramedic's eyes widened. He told the girl to speak with a nearby officer, then turned to Scout. "What did you see?"

Scout recounted the story, and Alex stepped away. He wandered around, looking for anyone else he knew.

All the kids looked shaken, though none as bad as Scout. Maybe, just maybe, that meant the deaths had been limited. Perhaps it had only been the school nurse. But from the news stories he heard about, the shooters rarely left only one victim in their wake.

Alex shook the thought from his head and continued wandering. One woman sitting in the back of an ambulance had blood splatter across her face and shirt. She seemed free of injury, though. It was probably the nurse's blood.

She'd been in the office. Maybe she'd seen Zoey.

Alex's heart leaped into his throat, and he sprinted over to her. "Did you see Zoey Carter? Ariana Nakano's mom?"

A paramedic grabbed Alex's arm. "You need to leave."

He yanked his arm away and kept his focus on the woman. "Did you see Zoey?"

"Go back to the front!" The paramedic squeezed Alex's shoulder and glared at him. "Now."

Alex pulled away, then turned back to the woman. "Did you?"

She shuddered, not making eye contact.

The paramedic stepped toward Alex, again.

"I'm leaving." Alex stormed away, fuming. That woman might

know if Zoey was okay. Would it have been so hard to let her answer the question? Just one question.

Alex rounded the corner of the building and froze mid-step. He recognized a face in the crowd. It didn't belong to a parent or a student.

That was a face Alex could never forget. One that still haunted his dreams.

Flynn Myer, the man who had abducted his daughter while Alex answered a work text. But Flynn was supposed to be in jail. No, he *was* in jail—without the possibility of parole.

So, how was it that Flynn stood only feet away from Alex? Sure, he had longer wavy hair, tanned skin, and blue eyes, but he had the face. The changes would've been easy enough to make.

Nobody else had that face.

TRAPPED

Ava opened her eyes. Not that it helped. It was pretty much just as dark as with her eyes closed.

She had a headache. It squeezed her skull and made her brain hurt.

Where was she? How had she gotten there?

A flood of memories ran through her mind. She'd been in the bathroom. Dave had come in, bearing guns.

Then he'd taken her to a janitor closet and put a smelly cloth to her face. That was the last thing she could remember.

Now she was lying somewhere dark. She squirmed. And she was tied. Ropes dug into her arms, wrists, and ankles.

Her mom's ex-boyfriend had made sure she wouldn't get out. Anger raged through her. He was as crazy as his stupid son.

Ava's stomach knotted. He'd better not try what his son had. She'd find a way to kill him, tied up or not. No way would she let him take advantage of her like Mason had.

She squirmed and wriggled, unable to break free of the ties. Something dug into her side when she moved to the right.

Where had Dave put her? That stupid jerk. And more importantly, what did he have in mind to do later? Also, what about the other kids at school? Had he killed anyone, or just shot the gun to scare everyone? If that was the case, it had worked *and* he'd gotten what he'd obviously wanted—her.

She froze. What about Parker? He hadn't gotten to Parker too, had he?

"Parker? Are you here?" she whispered, not that it mattered. Her words came out a muffle because something covered her mouth.

She should've seen that coming.

Would her little brother survive an abduction? Sure, he played a tough guy, but it was more of a show for everyone else—to piss off their parents for splitting up and for kids at school to think he was cool. But the kid still liked building Lego models and playing babyish video games. He wasn't even a teenager yet.

If Dave had taken him, Ava would need to protect him. And why wouldn't Dave have taken both of them?

Her stomach dropped. What about Hanna? She was so little still. He wouldn't take her, would he? Go to the elementary school with the gun?

Ava would definitely have to kill Dave if he'd taken little Hanna. She just needed to free herself and get out of wherever she was. Take him by surprise.

She squirmed all the more, ignoring the ropes digging into her skin, and rolled around as best she could. There wasn't much room.

Something rumbled.

Ava froze, listening. It sounded like an engine.

Had Dave stuffed her in a trunk? Could he get any more cliché?

She fought all the harder, then lurched to the left as the car started moving.

Ava screamed, for all the good it did. She could barely hear herself. If she could get her mouth free, she'd yell and yell, just to drive him crazy.

He'd thought she was a brat when he'd been dating Mom. That man had seen nothing yet. He would regret taking her. Ava would make sure of that.

PURSUIT

Alex's nails dug into his palms as he stared at Flynn. Was he the shooter? Had he gone into the school after escaping jail to find Ariana, the one girl who had gotten away from him? He'd killed all the others, and now wanted to finish what he'd failed to?

Not on Alex's watch.

He reached into his sweatshirt for his pocket knife and held it discreetly so that nobody would see.

Then he marched straight for Flynn, the convicted child abductor and killer. Why else would he be hiding in the crowd, watching the hurt and scared children?

He probably thought it was the perfect place to snatch one. If not Ariana, any other girl would probably do.

Alex's pulse drummed through his body. He'd fought this man before, he could do it again. Before he could take another kid or figure out where Ari was and take her once more.

With each step Alex took, he drew closer to the madman. He'd dreamed of actually finishing the guy off but never thought he'd get the chance since the man was on death row.

How had he managed to escape? Shouldn't the prison holding the state's most violent offenders have escape-proof security? If a prisoner had gotten out, wouldn't that have been all over the news?

Flynn glanced Alex's way. Their gazes locked.

It took a moment, but recognition covered his expression. His eyes widened, then narrowed.

What did he expect? Not to see Alex? He should've known Alex would be there. That he would be the first person to hunt Flynn down.

He should've stayed where he had police protection and walls keeping him from the outside world.

Now he had none of that, and since Alex wasn't yet a cop or even a cadet, there was nothing stopping him from dishing out a little vigilante justice.

Flynn's eyes shifted to the left and right, but he couldn't run. People pressed against him on all sides. He had no choice but to deal with Alex.

He was trapped by a sea of parents. Others would side with Alex. Turn on a sick and twisted man who enjoyed hurting little girls.

Flynn shoved a woman with platinum blonde hair, then forced his way past a balding skinny man, and ran toward the front of the school.

Alex burst into a run. "Stop him!"

Some people looked, but nobody moved. They were like deer in headlights.

Alex ran faster, skidding on some gravel. He regained his footing, nearly dropping his knife in the process, and chased after Flynn.

The criminal must've spent his life working out in prison. He was fast. Flynn rounded the corner and disappeared. He reappeared when Alex went around, too.

Flynn was heading straight for the woods. They were still a little ways off, and Alex wasn't closing the distance between them. If anything, the space between them was growing.

"Stop him!" Alex's voice was a little shrill that time. He didn't care.

Someone needed to figure out what was going on and tackle the man before he reached the cover of the trees.

Finally, a heavy-set guy in a sorely out-of-style jogging suit jumped into action halfway between Alex and Flynn.

Flynn jumped over some shrubs and darted around rose bushes. It slowed him enough that Alex was able to close the distance, at least until he reached the plants.

Just as he passed the roses, Flynn disappeared into the woods.

The dude in the jogging suit stopped and gasped for air. "Who's that guy?"

Alex didn't stop. "Only a child predator!" He ran past him and into the woods.

The other man's footsteps sounded from behind.

Flynn was nowhere to be seen, and there were several paths leading in different directions.

Alex went straight ahead, ducking under low-hanging branches and jumping over exposed roots. He listened for the criminal but couldn't hear anything over the ragged sounds of his own breathing.

The path branched out in other directions, appearing more like a maze than anything else. It was like it was designed as an escape for a convict.

Alex's lungs burned, but he kept running. He wouldn't stop until he caught up with Flynn or his legs wouldn't take him any farther.

He raced down one path, then another and another until he was certain he'd gone in a figure-eight. After taking a different fork, he circled back to the jogger.

Alex stopped and gasped for air. "Did... you... see... him?"

The guy wiped sweat from his brow and shook his head. "He got away."

"Unbelievable." Alex leaned against a tree, his muscles aching and burning.

"That guy's a child predator?"

Alex nodded, still trying to catch his breath.

"Is he the shooter?"

"No… idea."

"I'll go tell one of the cops."

Alex just nodded, but he didn't think it would do any good. None of them had bothered to go after them and find out why they were chasing someone.

Once he was able to breathe normally again, Alex wove his way out of the woods and back to the school grounds.

Jogger dude was talking to one of the cops from another precinct. He pointed to Alex.

The officer waved him over.

Alex picked up his pace and told the officer what had happened, and who Flynn was. "He might be the shooter! We have to stop him!"

He nodded, then radioed in the information. Not even a minute later, a policeman and policewoman raced into the woods.

"Can I go?" Alex asked. "I need to check on someone." He still didn't know if Zoey had been there during the shooting.

The officer shook his head. "You need to stay here. I have to call about the suspect. You said he's a death-row inmate?"

"Yes." Alex slid his knife back into his pocket.

"I haven't heard anything about an escape. I'm going to have to find out if it's true."

Alex gritted his teeth. "I'm telling you, it's him!"

"Don't move." The officer stepped away and pulled out a cell phone, keeping his gaze on Alex.

"You're related to Ariana?" Jogger asked.

Alex flicked a nod, eyeing both the cop and the woods.

"Brother or something?"

He got that a lot, given that he'd only been fourteen when Ari had been born. "Birth dad."

The guy raised his eyebrows.

"It's a long story."

"I'll bet."

They stood in awkward silence until the officer returned, his mouth and eyes twisted into a scowl. He stepped close to Alex. "Your guy is still on death row. He didn't break out. He isn't here. Care to tell me what's really going on?"

Jogger dude looked at Alex like *he* was the sicko.

Alex gave the cop a double-take. "I *saw* him! That was the guy who abducted my daughter. It was him!"

The officer shook his head. "Nope. He's reading War and Peace on his bed as we speak."

"That can't be."

"Oh, it is. It makes me wonder what you're up to, though. Why are you trying to distract us from what's going on here?"

Alex's mouth dropped open. "Are you kidding me?"

The cop pulled out a pair of cuffs from his jacket. "You're going to need to go downtown for questioning."

"You're not serious!" Alex stepped back. "You can't arrest me."

"I very much can." He arched a brow. "But I don't *have* to if you comply."

"Uh, can I go?" Jogger dude looked back and forth between the officer and Alex.

"Yeah. Thanks for your help."

Alex glared at the officer. "I'm no criminal. Talk to Captain Fleshman—he'll vouch for me."

"I don't know a Captain Fleshman."

"Detective Garcia? Anderson?"

"Nope. Not from around here. Give me your wrists, and I'll take you to the station for questioning."

Alex stuffed his hands in his pockets and stared him down. "I'm not leaving here in cuffs. You haven't arrested me! I'll go to the local station if I have to for questioning—in my own car, but you will *not* drag me away in handcuffs from my daughter's school. Do you understand?"

They stared each other down until the other man relented. "Okay. You definitely need to go in for questioning, but I won't arrest you. However, I'm going to your car with you and logging in all your information."

Alex bit back an angry retort. How could they waste time on Alex when they had a real suspect so close?

BOMB

Nick exited the classroom and turned to Foster. "That room's clear."

She nodded. "I just got word that the bomb squad is on its way."

"We'd better hurry. There's still a lot of ground to cover, and they're probably going to try and clear us out of here."

"They're coming from Seattle. That gives us a little more time, depending on when they left. Or maybe they're almost here already. I'm not sure."

"Okay. We're going to need all the time we can get." So far, they'd only found a few kids, but the last girl had been frightened out of her mind, just shaking in the corner of a classroom by herself. Foster had escorted her outside because she could barely walk on her own.

Nick and Foster continued checking classrooms for kids, but there didn't appear to be any down this hall. Someone else might've already cleared it earlier. It was hard to know, because this was hardly an organized scene.

It was actually one of the most chaotic Nick had seen in his career, and the fact that other forces came to help only added to the confusion. But it was better to be over-careful than under.

They reached the end of the hallway, and the only thing left was a janitor's closet. Nick nodded to it. "You want to check it out while I call it in that this section is clear?"

"Sure." Foster opened the door and stepped inside.

Nick pulled out his radio, and just as he was about to make the call, Foster poked her head out of the closet.

"You're going to want to see this." Her face was pale.

Nick's mind went wild with bloody images of kids as he leaped over to the closet.

Foster widened the door and stepped out of the way.

On the floor, in the middle of the tiny closet full of mops, brooms, and vacuums sat a rectangular black box with wires sticking out of every direction and several buttons on top.

They exchanged a worried glance. Foster pulled out her radio. "Is that the bomb?"

"If it isn't, someone really wants us to think it is." He reached for it.

Then he froze and stepped back, closing the door.

Beep.

Nick and Foster stared at each other, wide-eyed.

Beep, beep.

Foster pulled her radio out and called it in.

Nick reached for the door.

"Nick, no!"

He spun around, more from the surprise of her using his first name. Even during off-duty play dates with the kids, they'd really only ever called each other by their last names or rank.

"Don't open that door!" She pleaded with her eyes.

"You head outside. I'm going to check it out."

She shook her head. "I'm not going anywhere."

"Then step back." Nick turned around, giving her a moment to move, though he doubted she would. He grabbed the knob and his heart nearly exploded out of his chest.

The bomb—if that was what it was—might be connected to the door somehow. It hadn't made any noise until before he'd closed it.

"This is your last chance to step back," he warned her.

She didn't step away.

Nick flinched. He didn't want to be responsible for her death if the device really was a bomb. Nor did he want to put his own life on the line unnecessarily. He had three kids to think about.

"Captain?"

"Call it in. See if the bomb squad is close, or if we can talk to them. Find out what they say."

"Okay."

He turned around and faced the door. The beeping continued on the other side of the door. Nick's pulse pounded through his body. He really wanted to open that door, and being captain, it was his call. But at the same time, he had almost no experience with bombs. All the other times he'd dealt with them, they'd been fake. Given the severity of the situation as a whole, he had to be even more careful than usual.

Foster looked up from the phone at that moment and yelled, "They say we need to clear the building! Now!"

Nick turned around and met Foster's gaze.

Beep-beep-beep.

The noise was getting faster.

Without a word, they burst into a run down the hall. Nick glanced back several times, half-expecting to see a ball of flames headed their way.

Just as they neared the exit, the bomb squad came into view. They were covered in protective gear from head to toe, had several canines, and a large box—presumably to detonate the device.

Nick told them where it was, then opened the door, allowing

Foster to run out ahead of him. They ran through a courtyard, then down along another wing of the building until they came to the ball fields. The area was a sea of people and aid vehicles.

He stopped, scanning the crowd for his kids.

Foster skidded to a stop and turned to him. "Do you think this is far enough from the potential blast zone? Or should we tell everyone to leave the property?"

Nick took a deep breath. He didn't know enough about explosives to make an educated guess about the reach of the bomb—if that was in fact what they were dealing with. "We'd better let the experts make that decision. I don't want to see anyone getting hurt in a stampede to flee the school. That's likely the real danger."

"So, what do we do now?"

"Let's check on the rest of the scene. Find out what we know about the shooter and victims." That would give them the chance to walk around the perimeter of the building and would allow Nick to look for his kids.

DETAINED

Alex glared at the two-way mirror, though given how many people were at the school it was unlikely that anyone was bothering with him.

He tapped the scratched, inked table and read some of the scrawling others had written since his last visit to the room. It made his stomach knot thinking about how many times he'd been in these holding rooms over the years—usually when someone he cared about was missing. And here he was again, and Zoey was missing.

Alex wanted to throw up. How had he ended up back here? When he should be out there, searching for not only his fiancée but his daughter's abductor—the man who was supposedly behind bars in Walla Walla clear across the state.

It didn't make sense. Alex *knew* that face. He'd punched that face when Ari had been missing. They'd crossed paths while the coward was grocery shopping shortly after he'd taken Ariana. He'd been both bold and cowardly at the same time.

How could the guy be in two places at once? It made absolutely no sense. He couldn't be on death row and running free near a school shooting at the same time.

Yet there he'd been. Recognition had flickered on his face when he saw Alex. It was him.

Alex glowered at the mirror again. "How can you keep me locked up in here at a time like this?"

He got up and paced, shooting annoyed glances at the mirror every few seconds.

Had Flynn come back for Ariana? Did he take Zoey when he realized he couldn't get Ari? Or was it all a coincidence? Was he just there to see the show?

There were too many questions and not enough answers. Not any answers. And here Alex was, trapped in the tiny room unable to do anything to help anyone he loved.

For all he knew, Flynn was on his way to the Nakanos' to try and get Ariana but nobody would call over there and warn them because they didn't believe Alex. Just like they hadn't believed him before.

Would anything change after the academy? Once he was on the force, would they finally have some respect for him? Or would he always be seen as the town screw-up?

He went over to the door and pounded on it. "If you're going to hold me, at least make it worth the time! Don't just leave me in here!"

Alex flashed back to banging on another door. It had been a dirty room, and he'd been denied food.

He leaned against the door and closed his eyes. The filthy smell of that room came back to him. The taunts and the music. Not the music. That song played on loop for so long it still played in his mind at night when he couldn't sleep.

Alex spun around and hit the door again. "At least tell me if anyone has found my fiancée!"

It was pointless. Nobody was going to help him any more than back in that filthy cell.

Sighing, he sulked back over to the table and slunk into the same chair he'd been sitting in. He pulled off his sweatshirt, balled it up, shoved it on the table, and rested his head on it.

Alex closed his eyes, trying to ignore the song that would likely never leave him, and mulled over his interaction with Flynn. He let his mind run, hoping it would offer some clue he'd skipped over. Maybe he'd seen Zoey in the crowd, but he hadn't noticed because he'd been so focused on their daughter's abductor.

If he had, his memories weren't helping. Alex saw nothing new.

Just him sitting in the police station. Again. For someone who wasn't yet a cop, he'd spent too much time in these holding rooms.

He got up and paced again, for all the good it did him. What he needed was to be back at the school, looking for Zoey and their daughter's abductor.

How could Flynn be in two places at once? Nobody had believed Alex when he'd said he'd seen the guy back then, and they sure weren't listening now.

He glanced at the door again, but he wasn't going to act like a prisoner. Hitting the door and yelling wasn't going to get him the attention he wanted, not here and not back at his illegal cell.

Alex walked over to the mirror and stared at his own reflection, imagining who might be on the other side. Probably nobody, but it felt better thinking someone was there.

He knit his brows together. "What good is it keeping me here? Why am I being held? Because I said I saw someone? Give me a break! I haven't done anything wrong!" He glowered, picturing the small room back there, then walked the length of the mirror several times. "The only thing I did wrong was admit what I was doing. Clearly, you guys think I'm crazy. Why else would I be here? What are you going to do when I'm a part of this force? What then? Huh?"

Alex kept going for a while, but finally quit. It wasn't getting him anywhere. The chances of anyone being back there on a day like today were lower than low. Everyone was at the school. They'd just dropped him off and left. It wouldn't have surprised Alex if the fool hadn't even told anyone he was there.

He needed to talk to a lawyer about this, but they were holding his phone. As soon as Nick got back, Alex would demand to see him.

Nick knew Alex hadn't lost his mind. The police captain wanted him on the force. It was just a matter of Alex getting through the academy. Then they'd be golden.

Then it would be Alex's job to chase the criminals. He wouldn't get locked up for it.

"Let me out of here!"

CORRAL

Nick ran over to the last group of stragglers. "You need to leave the school grounds."

A lady with too much makeup glared at him. "Why?"

He gestured toward the bomb squad's well-marked vehicles. "There's a potential bomb. We're clearing the area."

She gave him a dramatic eye roll. "Fine, whatever. Come on, Conner." She put her arm around a kid and they headed away, the others with them following.

Nick jogged a little farther, coming to an officer from another force. "This area clear?"

"All clear. Any word on the device?"

"Not that I've heard. Now we need to get ourselves off the grounds."

The other officer nodded, and they headed across the street to where the crowds had gotten even bigger.

Word had probably spread far and wide about the shooting, and possibly the bomb threat. Now everyone in the area wanted a look for themselves.

Onlookers were inching closer. Nick ordered them back then told the officer with him to stay there and watch the people.

It was worse than trying to herd cats.

Nick walked around the perimeter, ordering the civilians to keep their distance while at the same time looking for his kids. His stomach twisted in knots.

He hadn't heard of any kids being shot, but that didn't mean there weren't any. This was the most disorganized crime scene he'd ever been to, especially with who-knew-how-many other departments on the scene and the bomb squad.

Nick continued telling people to stay back. It was amazing how many people were willing to risk their lives for the sake of curiosity. If there was a blast, debris would fly through the area they stood in. But considering how many fake bomb threats there were, it was no wonder next to no one was taking this seriously.

A loud crack sounded behind him. Nick spun around, aiming his gun toward the noise. A blinding flash of red and orange exploded from the part of the school where he and Foster had found the device. The noise was deafening for a moment, then the only sounds were of debris flying through the air, then landing.

People around him screamed and cried out. Others ran away, clutching kids. Some ran *toward* the building.

Nick stopped the ones he could, threatening arrest. Stabbing pains ran through his chest and he struggled to breathe.

It had been a real bomb. He and Foster had been right there.

If he'd tried to check it out, it could've killed them both.

Nick fought to take a deep breath. Everything moved in slow motion. He commanded people to stay back. Some ran away. Some stood, staring. Others just stepped back, never looking away from the scene.

Detective Garcia ran over. "Captain, what do we do now?"

"We need to keep these people back! For all we know, there are more of those devices around the rest of the building."

Garcia shouted at the crowd, who as a whole were inching closer.

Nick nodded to him. "I'm going to walk around."

"I'll stay here and keep these people back."

"Arrest anyone who doesn't listen." Nick glared at those who continued to inch closer to make sure they knew he meant business.

Then he headed back the direction he came, telling the scooters to stay back. All the while he struggled to breathe normally as he kept looking for his family.

When he rounded the block, he saw someone he knew.

Corrine.

His ex-wife who had moved his kids away across the country after divorcing him. She'd moved back with Parker after both their daughters moved back in with Nick.

Parker was with her now.

Nick's knees nearly gave out. Everything other than his son disappeared around him. For a moment, Nick was a father only, not a police captain. He burst into a run, pushed through the throng of people, and threw his arms around Parker. He squeezed him so tightly he risked crushing the boy's ribs.

He turned to Corrine, still clinging to their son. "Where's Ava? Hanna?"

Corrine just stared at him for a moment. Her face was pale, and her eyes held a terror he'd never seen in them before. She almost looked like a little girl herself.

"Corrine?"

She snapped out of it. "I haven't been able to find Ava. Hanna's school is under lock-down until further notice. I'm surprised you didn't know."

Nick lightened his grip on Parker. "I've been a little distracted."

"I figured."

"Speaking of, I have to get back to work. Call me the moment you hear anything about them."

Corrine nodded. "And you call me if you find Ava."

"I will." Nick squeezed Parker again, then kissed his face several times.

Surprisingly, Parker didn't push him away. In fact, he clung to Nick for a moment before stepping back. The boy's eyes shone with tears.

Nick squeezed his shoulder. "It's going to be okay."

Parker met his gaze. "Is it?"

"I'm going to do everything in my power to make sure it is."

"Just find Ava."

Nick cleared his throat. "I'll probably find her with her friends. You know how she is." He forced a smile.

Parker sighed and leaned against Corrine.

Nick hated to pull himself away. "I'll be back."

They both nodded, then Nick made his way back to the street and ordered more people to step back. It seemed that nobody cared about their own safety. Though he threatened arrests, there was no way they could incarcerate half the town. It just wasn't feasible.

He walked along the street slowly, keeping an eye out for Ava or any of her friends. Someone had to know where she was. All the other students had joined their families—or so it seemed.

Was Ava the only one that hadn't?

It certainly felt that way.

"Ava, where are you?"

TIED

Z oey Carter struggled against the ropes that held her to the chair. It didn't do any good—it would take a miracle for her to escape. The man had tied her wrists separately behind her back, her ankles were each tied to a chair leg, and even her waist was tied to the back of it.

She would scream if she could, but both the gag in her mouth and the duct tape across her mouth prevented her.

Her messy dark hair hung over her face and sweat beaded everywhere, dripping down her face, her back, her chest. Everywhere. It pooled in her bra.

The back of the chair dug into her bare skin, and the ropes burned. She'd been stripped down to only her ripped pants and a camisole.

She had half a mind to try and tip the chair over, but that didn't seem like it would help. It certainly wouldn't help her get out of the ties. Then she'd just be even more uncomfortable.

Not only that, but the little room was filthy. She'd probably end up with dirt in her eyes or scrape herself on an exposed nail from one of the loose floorboards.

Her stomach rumbled, despite her nerves. She hadn't eaten that morning. The plan had been to stop off at the school to get Ari's homework, then grab a quick bite on her way to work.

A gunman shooting up the school office hadn't been part of the plans.

Zoey shuddered as the scene replayed in her mind. She'd joked about something with the secretary, while she grabbed a file with Ariana's assignments. Then, mid-laugh, the man entered.

His eyes were wild. That'd been the first thing Zoey had noticed. Then he'd pulled out a gun.

She'd immediately ducked down and scrambled behind the desk.

Shots rang out. Blood sprayed. Some got onto her. The secretary fell, landing inches from Zoey. It had taken every ounce of her self-control not to scream. Not to cry. To just stay there quietly.

More shots. The school principal crashed to the ground not far from the secretary. Similar-sounding thuds around the room.

Zoey's eyes misted just thinking about it. The whole thing had been a nightmare. Except that it wasn't. It was as real as the dried blood on her clothes and face.

She closed her eyes, trying to push the memories away. It didn't work. The bodies fell before her closed eyes. Over and over again.

There was only one good thing about the whole ordeal— Ariana was safe at home, sleeping off the flu. She hadn't been there. She hadn't had to witness it. Experience the terror.

But she wouldn't be unscathed. Her school was no longer safe. She adored the secretary, who was now dead. The gunman might've shot some of Ari's friends. He'd taken her mom.

Zoey's heart shattered into a million pieces. Ariana had been through enough. More than enough. She'd gone through more horrors than someone four times her age.

That would be Zoey's focus. The one thing that would drive

her to get home in one piece. She needed to get back to her daughter before Ari ever found out Zoey had been taken in the first place.

She needed to get back home before Ariana recovered from the flu and found out what had happened. Zoey's parents—Ari's adoptive parents—would protect her from the news as long as possible. Hopefully it would be long enough.

The flu going around this year was keeping people down for a full two weeks. Ariana had only been sick since the night before. That would give Zoey more than a week to get back home before Ari was any wiser.

But how was she going to do that? What did the gunman have in mind for her?

Why hadn't he just killed her? Did he have something else planned? Or had he simply run out of bullets?

Zoey had waited under the desk, shaking and hardly able to breathe, for what felt like hours. In reality, it had only been about fifteen minutes according to the clock on the wall.

After stepping over the secretary and principal, she made her way around the bloody office, her heart nearly ready to explode out of her chest.

Shots rang out elsewhere in the building. Zoey picked up the phone from the desk and dialed nine-one-one. She glanced around for her purse, but it was the least of her concerns.

She needed to get out of the building, but not before calling for help. After telling the operator about the shooting and the dead bodies, she hung up before the woman on the other end of the line could tell Zoey to stay there until the officials arrived.

No way was that going to happen. She had every intention of getting outside, then running straight to her car.

Instead, the gunman appeared in the doorway again. Blocking her from escape. Not only that, but he had Ava with him. He held her by the hair, dragging the girl who looked unresponsive.

He'd locked his gaze on hers, then aimed his gun at Zoey's face.

Zoey had no time to react.

He pulled the trigger.

Nothing had happened.

The man swore profusely about the bullets. He reached into his pocket for more.

With his attention averted, Zoey ran toward him. She was going to grab Ava and run before he knew what had happened.

Instead, he dropped his gun and grabbed Zoey by the neck, squeezing so hard she couldn't breathe. He shoved her against the doorjamb. Her head hit hard enough that the sound bounced around between her ears.

By the time she regained her bearings, a different gun had been shoved in her face. "I may not be able to kill you just yet, but I'm sure not leaving you as a witness!"

From there, everything was a blur. He forced her outside to the back, screaming at her but letting her live.

Once they reached a sedan, he threw Ava into the trunk like a sack of potatoes before turning to Zoey. He continued his ravings, ordering her to her knees.

She complied.

"Take off your shoes!"

"What?"

He swung the gun. It hit her temple, giving her double vision.

Shaking, she removed her shoes.

"Now your socks!"

Zoey did that, too. Though she wanted to question him, she kept quiet. At least this was buying time. The police would be there momentarily.

"Your jacket!"

She complied again, wondering how far he was going to take it. Would she have to take off everything? Was he going to leave her there like that, or take her with him?

"Your shirt!" He moved the gun closer to her forehead, his finger on the trigger.

Zoey reached for the bottom of her blouse, her hands shaking. She fumbled with the lowest button.

"Faster!" He swung the gun in circles, moving closer to her face.

Barely able to think, she undid the bottom button, then the next one and the next. Tears blurred her vision as she continued until there were only three left.

Sirens.

His eyes widened. He swore. "Get in the car!"

Her mouth gaped.

"Get in!" He hit her with the gun again.

She scrambled to her feet, then fumbled with the handle and climbed in the back seat.

He shoved her to the floor. "You stay down, or you're getting a bullet in your head!"

Shaking violently, she nodded.

The door slammed shut, and before she knew it, he'd flung himself into the driver's seat and they'd squealed away.

A moment later, they passed a police cruiser and fire engine going to the school. The lights shone on the roof of the car.

They continued driving, and the farther they went, the more emergency vehicles they passed.

Zoey silently begged for someone to see her in the car.

Nobody did.

After a while—she had no idea how long, because time was passing so strangely—he stopped the car.

She had thought her heart couldn't pound any harder, but it did. As soon as the door flung open, she cried out, her voice eerily shrill, but she was ready to attack.

He still had the gun, and he aimed it at her again. Then he grabbed her by the collar and ripped off her shirt. She cried out in pain. Thankfully she'd decided to wear a camisole that morning. He didn't make her take that off.

He aimed the gun at her again, then tossed it aside before he pulled out the ties and duct tape. But tying her up, shoving a cloth in her mouth, and covering it with duct tape wasn't enough. He covered her from head to foot with a blanket before slamming the door and driving again.

FINALLY

Adoor slammed shut.

Alex bolted upright from the table. He wiped drool from his mouth and glanced toward the door.

A very tired-looking Nick stood there. "What the hell did you do this time, Alex?"

"I was chasing a potential shooter."

Nick rubbed his temples and sat across from Alex. "At the school?"

"Where else?" Alex held his gaze. "I was looking for Zoey."

Nick gave him a double-take. "Zoey?"

"Ariana's home sick, and she went to collect Ari's homework. I take it you didn't see Zoey."

"No. Can't find Ava, either."

"Oh, Nick. I'm so sorry."

He gave a little nod. "She—and now Zoey—are the only ones unaccounted for. I didn't know Zoey was there. Was she near the office, by chance?"

"I'd assume so."

"She's lucky, then. We didn't find her, and that's where all the dead bodies were. Our shooter only went after adults. All the kids are safe and sound. Ava's the only one we can't find." Nick rubbed his temples again and rested his head in his hands.

"I'm so sorry, Nick."

"We're still interviewing kids, but I had to leave once the building was cleared of any more potential bomb threats. Once again, I'm too involved to be part of an investigation."

"Isn't everyone on the force involved in some way?" Alex pressed his palms on the table. "I mean, this isn't a big town. Everyone has to know someone who either goes to the school or works there."

Nick glanced up at Alex, shadows darkening his eyes. "Yeah, but nobody else is related to the only missing student."

"Would she have been taken?"

Nick groaned. "It's either that or she's scared, hiding some-where. That's what I keep hoping."

"Maybe Zoey's with her. She'll take care of Ava."

Nick didn't respond.

They sat in silence until Alex spoke. "So, can I leave? I've been in this room for hours. I have to piss so bad, I've been tempted to use the corner."

"Why are you here, again?" Nick rubbed his eyes.

Alex squirmed in his seat, his bladder burning. "I thought I saw someone suspicious, so I ran after him. He got away, and some turkey from another force thought I needed to be held for ques-tioning."

Nick arched a brow. "That makes no sense."

"That's what I've been saying all along. Can I use the bathroom, or should I use the corner?"

"Go. Just don't leave the building."

"No problem." Alex jumped from the chair, practically flew across the room, then raced to the bathroom. He made it to the urinal just in time, and he closed his eyes as relief washed through him.

When he was finally done, he saw Nick in his office. The door was cracked open, so Alex walked in.

Nick glanced up from his laptop. "I was about to send in a search party."

"I told you I had to go."

Nick gestured to the chair on the other side of the desk. "What made you think the guy you chased was a suspect?"

Alex's stomach twisted in a knot, but he sat.

"What?" Nick closed his laptop and locked Alex's gaze.

"He was Flynn Myer."

Nick's brows came together. "You do realize he's in Walla Walla, right?"

"It was *him*. I'd know that face anywhere—no matter how well disguised."

Nick closed his eyes for a moment. "Alex, don't do this. Not now."

"I can't help the timing! You remember what happened last time. I kept saying I saw him, and nobody believed me. Look who was right."

Nick sighed. "Flynn Myer has no chance of parole. He hasn't escaped—I'd be the first to hear about that, being that I lead the force where he was captured. He lived here."

"Exactly why he'd come back here. I'm telling you, it was him. He even recognized me."

Nick tilted his head. "Really?"

"Yes! I'd swear on my own life."

"Okay, here's what we'll do."

Alex leaned forward, eager to hear.

"I'll have you speak with the sketch artist. Just don't tell anyone you think it's Flynn."

"But it's him!"

"Let the professionals figure that out. I don't want you telling anyone else. Don't give anyone reason to question your sanity."

Alex glared at his friend. "I'm right. They'll figure it out."

Nick pulled his laptop back up and started typing. A minute later, he glanced back over at Alex. "Myer's still in prison. He's one of their best-behaved inmates, so he gets to help cultivate some plants. Don't tell anyone you think you saw him. Stick to the story that you were running after who you thought was the shooter."

"I was! And it's him. Flynn goes after kids. Young teen girls." Alex held Nick's gaze.

"Our shooter only killed adults."

Alex leaned forward. "Ava's missing. What if he has her?"

Nick took a deep breath. "Was she with him when you chased him?"

"No."

"Ava probably ran off, scared. She already has some issues she was dealing with from when she lived across the country."

"Corrine's ex-boyfriend's kid?"

Nick nodded.

Alex remembered that drama. That kid had been nothing but trouble.

Nick took a deep breath. "I need to hang up my captain hat for a while and try to find my daughter. The sketch artist is at the elementary school, talking to people there."

"Not the middle school?"

"The middle school building is clear but unsafe. Plus, there's a lot to process."

Alex rose. "Does this mean I'm free?"

"Yeah. Get out of here."

"Don't I have paperwork to fill out?"

"You were just being held for questioning, and whoever brought you here barely even mentioned you were there."

Alex grumbled under his breath as he headed for the door. He turned around. "I hope you find Ava soon."

"Thanks. And same with Zoey."

"Hey, if you want to talk, I'm here."

Nick nodded. "I just want to get out there and look until she's in my arms, safe and sound."

Alex knew that feeling all too well.

CONTRAST

Alex slammed his car door and closed his eyes. Giving his description of Flynn to the artist had been a complete waste of time.

His sketch looked nothing like any of the other drawings of the gunman. All of them were skinny with longish hair, but that was where the similarities ended. Flynn had wavy dark hair, light eyes, and a tired look about him. The other sketches all had light hair, dark eyes, and totally different features.

Flynn stood out among all the other drawings. He couldn't be the gunman, but why had he been at the school? Just to watch, so he could pick out his next victim?

Alex's phone buzzed. It had been going off the entire time he'd been inside the elementary school.

He pulled it out of his pocket and fought to open his eyes. There were an array of calls, from both his relatives and Zoey's.

What did they think he could offer? He didn't know where she was, either.

Alex called his dad back. He hadn't spoken with his parents since all of this started.

"Alex, where have you been?" Dad answered.

"Trying to find Zoey. How's Ari, do you know?"

"She's really sick, but at least safe in her bed. We just brought over some soup. Kenji and Valerie are a mess. Valerie's beating herself up for not going to the school instead of sending Zoey. Mom's over there, talking with her now. Have you found anything on Zoey?"

Alex ran his fingers through his hair. "I wish. She and Ava have disappeared without a trace."

"Ava? As in, Nick's daughter?"

"Yeah, they're both gone. No clues for either of them. Not yet, anyway. They still have to process the entire school. I have no idea how long that will take. I hate this."

"We're worried out of our minds, too. Zoey's like a daughter to us. Let us know if you hear anything, or if we can help."

Alex groaned. "I wish there was something to do. If there was, I'd be doing it right now."

"Maybe you should get some rest. You can come here, you know. Your old room is always open."

"Thanks, Dad. I'll probably just crash at my place, not that I can see myself getting much sleep."

"Try. You're going to need your rest."

Unfortunately, Alex knew that all too well. "I will. Oh, wait. How's Macy?"

"Good, and we haven't told her about Zoey. She could go into labor any day now, and this news could make it start early. If you talk to her, don't mention it."

"I won't. Tell me the moment she's headed to the hospital. I want to be there."

"Hopefully Zo will be back by then. Macy wants both of you there to meet the baby."

A lump formed in Alex's throat. "Send her our love." His voice cracked. "Love you, Dad."

"We love you, Alex. Our offer to stay stands day or night. Come over at any hour."

Tears misted his eyes. "Thanks. Talk to you later."

Alex ended the call before he ended up breaking down. He cleared his throat and blinked back the threatening tears. Then he started the ignition. One thing he could do was to drive around town.

The first place he went was the middle school. It was lit up as though school were in session. Police cruisers, ambulances, and fire trucks were scattered throughout the parking lot. The entire parking lot was blocked off with yellow tape.

More than anything, Alex wanted to run over and help process the scene. But even if he was a cop, he wouldn't be allowed in. With a missing fiancée, he was too involved—just like Nick.

Alex's stomach twisted in tight knots. He drove around the property and nearly skidded off the road when he saw the part that had blown up. Half the wall was missing, exposing the classrooms inside. Bricks lay clear across the parking lot and had broken several car windows.

If anyone had been in there at the time, there was no chance of survival.

Whoever had done all of this was one sick bastard. Shooting up a school, then blowing it up. For what? Why would anyone do that?

Alex gripped the steering wheel so hard his knuckles turned white. Whether it was Flynn Myer or some other twisted piece of garbage, Alex hoped he got to the coward before the cops—especially if he'd abducted Zoey and Ava in addition to everything else. He'd make sure the loser paid in ways the justice system never could.

A horn honked behind him.

Alex waved an apology and drove around the rest of the school until he reached the woods where he'd gone after Flynn. He slowed and stared, then picked up speed so as not to irritate the person behind him again.

He drove around the surrounding neighborhoods. The only thing out of the ordinary were the extra patrols. Cops were everywhere.

Good. Maybe they'd actually find the guy, or better yet, Zoey and Ava. As much as Alex didn't want to think about it, the only thing that made any sense was that the shooter had taken them hostage. That meant that Flynn was only a looky-loo, and that actually matched his profile—that of a sick coward.

But who had shot up the middle school, and what did they want with Ava and Zoey?

Alex's mind mulled over the many possibilities as he drove farther from the school. He was about to turn back around when something white on the sidewalk caught his attention.

He pulled up to the curb and glanced over. It was something almost like a ball, but it was also partially spread out in one direction.

Alex turned on the hazard lights and got out. The closer he got to the thing, the more it looked like a piece of clothing. He stopped and studied it, his feet just inches from it.

His heart skipped a beat when he recognized the buttons. They were silver with something painted on them in black.

He whipped out his cell phone and used it as a flashlight to get a better look. The buttons had the Eiffel Tower painted on them.

It was one of Zoey's favorite work shirts. She adored the city of love, and they were saving to go there for their first anniversary.

Something else on the shirt caught his attention. Red splotches.

Heart thundering, he knelt and angled his phone. Blood spatter decorated part of the collar and an arm.

Alex fell to the ground, trying to breathe.

It was Zoey's shirt. Zoey's bloody shirt. Where was she? Why wasn't it on her?

He reached for it, but then stopped.

Zoey's shirt was evidence. As much as he wanted to hold it close and smell her perfume, he couldn't touch it. Not when it could help lead them to the killer.

Alex turned off the flashlight function and called the station.

FRETTING

Genevieve Foster kissed the top of Tinsley's head. "Sweet dreams."

The girl held her gaze for a moment before closing her eyes.

Genevieve brushed some hair away from Tinsley's forehead before leaving the room. She kept the door open just a crack. It had been a few weeks since Tinsley had woken from a nightmare, but that didn't mean it couldn't happen again.

Before coming to her, the girl had been through hell. Her parents had both been criminals. First her dad died, then her mom forced her to help her abduct men then torture them. Tinsley may have even seen some of them die. Nobody knew, because Tinsley was tight-lipped about everything, even to her counselor and Genevieve—two of the only people she would talk to.

It had been months, but still Tinsley clung to her, rarely talking. But that was more than she gave most people.

Genevieve poured herself a glass of white wine, then settled on the couch. Her head pounded from the day's stress.

When she'd watched part of the middle school explode, she

had nearly collapsed. That could've been her and Captain Fleshman.

Her heart raced, but not because of the bomb. Because of the image of her boss's face. It was nothing short of a miracle that she could speak a coherent sentence in his presence. Every time she saw him, her throat nearly closed up and her pulse pounded through every inch of her body.

He was not only so handsome it should be illegal, but he was sexy as hell. The shirts he wore, especially the V-neck tees he wore off duty, showed off the fact that he had to live at the gym.

Then there was the way he looked at her. He could knock her to the floor with just one glance.

She'd thought she'd imagined it for the longest time—that she was just some pathetic lovesick puppy. The new girl on the force, fresh out of the academy, falling for the head of the department. But then when she visited him in the hospital, there was no more denying the electricity in the air between them. It was so thick, she could barely breathe.

After Tinsley came to stay with her, and the captain suggested they get their kids together, there was even less she could do to deny their mutual feelings for each other.

She closed her eyes and imagined pressing herself against him and giving him a kiss that would surely get her fired.

It was so hard to know what to do. On one hand, working with him was building her career faster than it could without him. She was rising through the ranks faster than most, and she learned so much from him every time they went out on a call.

Yet at the same time, Genevieve didn't know how much longer she could keep her feelings at bay. One of these days, she was bound to grab his hand and thread her fingers through his, or worse, act upon the things she imagined doing to him in her mind. Career-killing things if anyone ever found out.

She couldn't do anything to risk either of their jobs. Maybe once she made Sergeant, she could look into switching to a nearby force. It wouldn't be the same without Nick there, but if they could finally pursue what they both so clearly wanted, it would be worth it.

Coming home to see him at the end of the day would by far beat seeing him at the station.

Guilt stung her for thinking about this now of all times. With his daughter missing, romance would be the last thing on his mind.

What she needed to do was call and see how he was doing. Find out if he needed anything. Not that she could get anything now. She had to be home in case Tinsley woke up. It would traumatize the poor girl to wake up and discover she was alone.

Genevieve finished off her glass of wine, then pulled out her phone. She brought up the captain's contact information. His smiling face took her breath away.

What she wouldn't give to press her mouth on those lips.

Focus. Despite the happy photo on her screen, the man was suffering in real life. In the worst way possible. What could be worse than having something horrible happen to your kid?

She had been a complete wreck after her cat died. Something involving a child had to be a million times worse.

Genevieve pressed call and waited as it rang. She was about to hang up before it went to voicemail, but he answered.

"Foster?"

Her heart jumped into her throat at the sound of his deep voice. It took her a moment to recover. "How are you holding up?"

He groaned. "Barely. I'm trying to sleep but can't. I close my eyes, but all I see is Ava in trouble."

The pain in his tone broke her heart. "Can I do anything?"

"We need to find them. But I can't do anything. I'm off the case."

Genevieve sat taller. "I'll do everything I can, Captain. Everything in my power. I'll work harder on this case than anything ever before." She grimaced. That was a bit much.

"I appreciate it."

At least he hadn't noticed. "Do you want to discuss the case? We can talk about every angle."

"I don't know what I want."

"Maybe talking about it will help us see something we missed before."

"Maybe."

Silence rested between them. Her mind raced as she tried to think of something helpful to say. But what would help in a situation like this?

"You know what's the worst?" he asked.

"What?"

"Aside from not knowing where Ava is, I mean. It's being alone. Parker and Hanna are with Corrine this week. It's probably for the best, as I'm in no shape to even take care of myself and I'm going to have to be at work a lot."

"Come over here." Her eyes widened. She hadn't meant to say that. Her heart pounded so hard, it was the only thing she could hear. The only times the two of them had gotten together off the clock was for the kids' playdates.

More silence. Crap. What if she'd completely misread all of his signals? Or worse, he thought seeing her was a bad idea? She scrambled to find something to say.

He spoke first. "You really mean that?"

Genevieve took a deep breath to steady her voice. "Yeah. Are you hungry? I can fix something."

"I'd like that. I haven't eaten since before the shooting."

He actually wanted to come over? "Okay, I'll throw something together."

"Thanks, Genevieve. It really means a lot."

Her breath caught at him calling her by her given name.

ROOM

Ava sat up, gasping for air. She glanced around the dim room. It was a tiny dusty bedroom.

She tried to remember how she'd gotten there from the trunk. Then she remembered. Dave had shoved another smelly cloth to her face, making her pass out.

That jerk!

But he'd taken the ties off her wrists. She was free! Free to sneak up on him and hit him over the head with something heavy.

Ava jumped from the bed, lunging for the door. She crashed straight down to the hardwood floor. Her hip, elbow, and chin all hit first. Then the breath knocked out from her chest.

As she struggled to breathe again, she sat up and felt her ankles.

Handcuffs. And they were tied to the bed. Probably with the same rope that had been around her in the car.

The door flung open and banged against the wall. Dave stood there, glaring at her, his hands pressed against the frame. "I see you woke up."

"Let me go!"

"Is that any way to talk to the one person who can bring you

59

food and water?"

"Why did you do it? Shoot the school and take me? Do you have Parker or Hanna?"

"You always did talk too much. Shut up!"

Ava flinched. She'd forgotten how loud he got when angry. His voice was like a weapon.

"Just to let you know, things'll go a lot easier for you if you're agreeable."

Her defenses shot up. "Agreeable to what, exactly?"

"Everything." Dave stepped closer to her, slow and exacting. He wanted to intimidate her, and it was working.

Not that she was going to let him know that. She straightened her back and tried to stand. The handcuffs and short rope made it challenging, but not impossible. "What are you going to do to me?"

He stopped and stared at her, eye to eye, barely having to lower his head. "You've gotten taller."

"And smarter. And stronger."

"You'll never be smarter than me."

"You wish."

"Do you remember what I said about being agreeable?"

She put her hands on her hips. "When do you ever recall me being agreeable?"

He laughed cruelly. "I can think of one time."

When Mason had taken advantage of her. "What do you want?"

"We'll talk later. After you've had some time to think about what I said."

Ava clenched her fists. "Just let me go. I won't tell anyone it was you, okay? Not at the school, and not the one taking me. I'll say I never saw your ugly face."

Dave shoved her, and she fell back against the bed. He loomed over her, his nostrils flaring. "Think about what I said."

She struggled to sit upright. "Do you have Hanna and Parker?"

"If I do, you'd better change your attitude!" He spun around and left, slamming the door.

"Still a spineless jerk," she muttered.

But what if he did have her brother and sister?

Why would he take any of them? To try and get Mom back? Like that would ever happen. Or was he trying to make her pay for leaving him? Maybe it was because his kid got in trouble for copping a feel under Ava's shirt at that party?

Both Dave and Mason were spineless jerks who thought the world owed them.

Her stomach rumbled.

Great. Ava scowled. That was what Dave was going to use against her to get her to do what he wanted—whatever that was. *He* sure wasn't going to feel her up.

Unless he already had, when she'd been unconscious. Her stomach lurched at the thought, but she wouldn't put it past him. Like father like son, right?

Well, not while she was awake. No way was that happening. Her arms were free, so she could fight him off.

Ava swung her feet up on the bed and studied the cuffs. They looked like the real deal. Her dad was a cop, so she'd seen plenty of real ones. Dad had even let her play with them and try to get out so she could see how impossible they were to get out of. She'd fought and struggled, and even broke into a sweat before he finally unlocked them.

As soon as she got away from Dave, she was going to demand Dad teach her to use a gun. He wouldn't turn her down, not after this.

She took a deep breath. It was a matter of getting away, and that would start with getting the rope untied from handcuffs. Then she'd have to find the key—hopefully Dave had it—then she could make her escape.

It would take some time. The knot looked complicated and majorly tight. It would take a while.

But she had nothing other than time.

OVERWHELM

Nick pulled into the parking spot. It took three tries to get his Mustang in straight. He probably shouldn't have had that last beer. Or at least not gotten into the car after downing it.

It wasn't like it had helped him to forget the fact that nobody knew where Ava was. His firstborn was missing, potentially with a killer. It would take being knocked unconscious to forget this living nightmare.

He wanted to strangle someone in their little town. Why didn't that school have security cameras? Nick would make sure that changed. He'd take it straight to the mayor if he had to.

All they had were drawings from the sketch artist. Unless someone at school had snapped a picture. Kids these days were so obsessed with their phones, surely *one* of them had gotten a photo of the guy.

But they had been scared for their lives. When going through the building, he saw at least a dozen abandoned cell phones strewn about. For kids to leave them, they had to have been terrified.

Nick turned off the car and double-checked Foster's apartment number. At least they would be able to talk openly about the case. They were away from the station.

Maybe she knew something important. That could be why she called him. Or had he called her?

He really shouldn't have had that last beer.

Too late for that now. Nick climbed out of the car, stumbled back, then set the alarm. He glanced around. The other cars were nice enough. Nobody would probably mess with his prize possession.

He shoved more breath mints into his mouth and meandered toward the building. Hopefully the coffee and energy drink he'd downed after talking to Foster would kick in soon to give him some clarity of mind. So far, they'd only given him the jitters.

After Nick found her apartment, he leaned against the door and took a deep breath. He needed to pull himself together if he didn't want Foster to think he'd gotten drunk.

He'd spent too much time trying to impress her to blow it now. But if something horrible happened to his daughter, would he even be capable of having a relationship after that? His throat closed up at the thought. Or maybe he'd need one more than ever. There was really only so much he could do on his own.

He'd really made a name for himself. Some of the guys at the station called him the Lone Ranger because he'd gone so long without a relationship after his marriage fell apart. They were right, though. He should've moved on a long time ago.

And now he was. Foster was gorgeous. The blue uniform that muted everyone else couldn't hide her good looks—not even that could suppress her beauty and feminine curves.

Nick's pulse raced at the thought. He stepped away from the wall and knocked, careful not to be too loud since Tinsley had to be sleeping at this hour.

Only about half a beat passed before the lock clicked and the door opened. Foster stood there with her hair down, flowing halfway to her waist. She wore a pale yellow sleeveless dress that was just short enough to quicken his heart rate.

She stepped back. "Come on in. Brr. It's chilly out here."

Nick went inside, careful to keep his steps steady, and hung his jacket on a coatrack. It slid off the hook, but he caught it and shoved it so that it stayed while she had her back to him, locking the door.

She turned around and gave him a sad smile. "How are you holding up?"

"It's rough."

Foster nodded and walked down the hall. He followed her as they passed the kitchen and came to the living room. She gestured for him to sit on the couch. "Can I get you anything? Water?"

Nick shook his head. If he had anything else to drink, he'd have to get up to pee every five minutes. "Maybe something to eat?"

"I made you enchiladas. Or is that too heavy? I can get you a light snack, if you'd rather."

She was like an angel. Nick hadn't had someone make him a homemade meal in months, and that was only because he'd been at his parents' house. "Whatever's easiest."

"It's all easy." She smiled sweetly.

Nick's breath caught. "Uh, enchiladas sound great."

"Sure. Give me a few minutes. Have a seat." She waved toward the couch. "You can change the channel if you want."

He stumbled over to the couch, plopped down, then glanced at the screen. The Hallmark Channel. Everyone has their poison. He grabbed the remote from the coffee table and flipped through the channels, stopping at an action flick. Two guys in a fistfight. Much better.

Just as the fistfight resolved itself, the delicious aromas of the meal wafted his way. Nick's mouth watered.

Foster strolled over, carrying two steaming plates, though one had less food on it. Her dress moved up ever so slightly with each step. Nick pulled his gaze away from her tan legs to her face. She smiled at him with her full lips.

Not helping.

He licked his lower lip and took a deep breath. "Those smell delicious."

Foster's expression lit up and she set them on the coffee table. "I hope you like them. It's an authentic recipe from a friend who spent a year in Mexico."

Nick tried not to stare as she bent over. He wasn't very successful. "Um, I'm sure they're great."

She stood up straight. "Let me grab something to drink. Dig in."

He just nodded, entranced by the perfect shape of her mouth. And of the rest of her.

Coming over was either the best decision or the worst. Only time would tell which was true.

She spun around and bounced toward the kitchen. The dress again rose and lowered with each step.

Once she disappeared from sight, Nick turned to the food. All of a sudden, he realized just how hungry he actually was. He inhaled one full enchilada before Foster returned, carrying two pop cans with writing in Spanish.

"I like to drink authentic Mexican soda with these."

"Where do you get those?"

"There's a little shop not far away. They have all kinds of authentic ingredients."

"You're amazing. I mean, this meal is incredible."

Foster beamed, handed him a can, then sat next to him. She smelled like a tropical island. "Thanks. How do you like it?"

He struggled to find his voice. "It's better than any restaurant I've ever been to."

"You can have as much as you want. There's plenty more where that came from."

Nick nodded and turned back to his plate. Tingles ran through his body. He could barely think straight with her next to him. Or was that because of the beers he'd consumed before coming over?

It didn't matter. He needed to get his mind on the food and off how much he wanted to kiss her until he forgot his problems completely.

CONNECTION

Genevieve struggled to eat her meal. It was hard enough to breathe with him sitting so close. He was wearing one of his V-neck tees. This one seemed to cling to him more than the others.

It was hard not to stare. Not to let her mind take it off.

Stop! He was grieving and stressed out. His daughter was missing. Not only that, but they had both been through one of the worst work days possible.

It had definitely been her worst day on the job. Nick had been on the force a lot longer than her—probably since she was a preteen or young teen. That thought made her heart race even faster. He was so much older and more experienced with the world. That combined with the way he looked at her... it all made eating nearly impossible.

"You mind watching this?" Nick asked.

"It's fine." She hadn't even noticed the TV. Buildings exploded on the screen. After seeing part of the school blow up earlier, it made her flinch.

"Yeah, probably not the best choice for today." He balanced the plate on his lap and turned the channel until he came to an old episode of *Supernatural*. "This better?"

"Sure. I love this show."

Nick turned and met her gaze. "You do?"

She swallowed, getting lost in his light brown eyes. "It's one of my favorites."

"Mine, too."

Time seemed to stand still as their gazes remained locked. She studied the dark flecks in his irises, her skin warming with each moment that passed. She wanted to lean over and press her lips on his.

Something inside her screamed that he was her boss.

But she didn't care. She would throw it all away just to taste that mouth. She leaned forward.

Nick pulled back and turned toward the TV.

Genevieve closed her eyes. Her pulse drummed in her ears. She shook so hard she had to put her plate on the coffee table.

What had she almost just done? No wonder Nick had pulled away. They couldn't kiss. She wasn't just risking her job, but his. Not only that, but he was distraught and had clearly had some drinks before coming over. This was not the time.

She drew in several deep breaths until she stopped shaking.

On screen, a piano fell on Dean.

Nick burst out laughing. "This is my favorite episode! How many times can they kill him?"

His laughter made Genevieve feel better, and relaxation washed through her. She smiled. "This is one of the funnier ones."

Nick put his plate next to hers, and they laughed their way through the rest of the episode.

Once it ended, he turned to her, his eyes full of sadness. "I really needed to laugh."

She put her hand on his, then froze when she realized the gesture.

He didn't indicate that he was put off by it.

"Do you want me to find more episodes? We can watch the funny ones all night if you want."

The sadness in his expression deepened. "It wouldn't be right to laugh all night while Ava's out there, missing, would it?"

Genevieve frowned. "I don't know."

He leaned against the couch and raked his fingers through his hair. "I feel guilty for enjoying myself, but if I don't laugh, I think I'll fall apart."

She nodded, feeling his crushing pain. "You have to take care of yourself. It's the only way you can help to find her."

"You're right." He lifted his hand that rested under hers and threaded his fingers through hers.

Her heart pounded, threatening to explode through her chest.

Nick took her other hand and traced shapes on her palm. "I like being around you. I can let my defenses down and just be myself. There's no need to pretend to be anything I'm not."

She opened her mouth, but no words came.

He leaned forward and pressed his mouth on hers. His lips were rough, like they were chapped, but it was like Heaven. Her insides exploded with joy, and immediately, he deepened the kiss. Their tongues danced and explored.

It was even better than she'd imagined.

His grip on her hands loosened, and she ran her palms up his arms. He flexed, showing her just how good of shape he was in. Her heart nearly exploded. Their kiss intensified as she continued exploring his arms, then his equally solid chest and abs.

Nick's hands moved to her waist, then to the small of her back. He pulled her closer, pulling her onto his lap and pressing her against him. His hands made their way up to her dress's zipper. He slid it down a few inches.

Then he pulled back.

Genevieve's eyes flew open. "What's wrong?"

"Is this okay?" He sounded breathless.

"It's more than okay."

Nick's expression intensified. "Is it?"

She nodded. "I won't tell anyone. Nobody else will ever know. I swear."

He leaned forward, like he was going to kiss her again, but then stopped. "I need you. Like I've never needed anything in all my life."

Genevieve put her palms on his face and pressed her mouth on his. He deepened the kiss and moved his hands back to her zipper.

RELIEF

Alex paced the waiting room in the police station. At least it was better than being in one of the holding rooms.

Detective Anderson appeared. "Come on back, Alex."

"Where's Nick?"

Anderson rubbed his eyes. "At home, sleeping."

Alex followed him to his cubicle, his mind racing. "What can you tell me about Zoey's shirt? Is it her blood?"

"Sit." The detective gestured toward the seat, then sat on the other side of the desk.

Alex sat. "What do you know?"

"First of all, DNA evidence takes longer than an hour. The shirt probably hasn't even reached Seattle yet, where it has to be processed."

"You guys still don't have a lab here? Even with all the crap that goes wrong around here?"

"Talk to your buddy. He's the captain."

Alex scowled. "Why would Zoey's shirt be lying on the sidewalk? Why?"

"Take a deep breath."

Alex leaned forward. "How would you feel if this was your fiancée?"

"It's too soon to know anything, Alex. But I *can* tell you one thing that will put your mind at ease."

"What?"

"Looking at the shirt, I can tell you it's not her blood."

It took Alex a moment to find his voice. "What? How do you know that?"

"I know enough about blood spatter to tell you that based on the direction of the spray, it came from someone else. She was near someone who bled onto her."

"Are you sure?"

Anderson nodded. "And if you need more convincing, the blood was on the outside of the shirt."

Alex crumpled against the chair. "So, she's not bleeding?"

"Not when she had the shirt on, anyway."

His mind raced as he tried to piece everything together. "But that still doesn't tell me why her shirt would be there, bloody or not. I can't imagine her just throwing it there."

"That's where we're going to need you to be patient. It's going to take time to process everything."

Patience, right.

Alex sat up straight and stared at the detective. "How did the shooter get away?"

Anderson frowned. "He fled the scene before anyone arrived."

"How is that possible? That never happens on the news stories."

"It does. Believe me, it does."

Alex would just have to take his word. His mind was swimming too furiously for him to think about other school shootings. At least it sounded like Zoey was alive.

That was all that mattered. Well, that and Ava being okay. They were both missing.

"Any other questions?" Anderson asked.

Alex groaned. There were at least a million questions racing through his mind. "Do you guys know who the shooter is yet?"

"It's going to take time."

"There are two lives on the line!" Alex slapped his hands on the sides of the chair.

Anderson glared at him. "We *know* that. Our captain's daughter is one of them! I've worked with Captain Fleshman since you were a smart-mouthed little brat when your sister was missing. He's more of a brother to me than my own brother. I'm going to put everything I have into this case, and lucky for you, that includes working to find your fiancée. Why don't you head home and get some sleep, Alex? Let us do our job. I'm sure as hell not getting any sleep tonight."

Alex just stared at the other man who would one day be his superior. He was rarely at a loss for words. Alex nodded and rose from his chair.

His mind reeled from being chewed out, but he probably had it coming. He had a lot to learn about being a cop, and if he wanted any respect when he joined the force, he needed to get his act together now. Most of the people there had seen him at his worst, either when his sister or his daughter had been kidnapped.

Now his fiancée, the one and only love of his life, had potentially been abducted, too. What were the chances? Was there something about him that made it dangerous for others to be around?

The chances of that many people he cared about disappearing had to be astronomically low. Just about as close to impossible as it came.

He slammed his car door shut but didn't start the engine. Macy had disappeared right after he'd started smoking and making out with her best friend. Ariana had disappeared when Alex's life was at its lowest.

Had he done something wrong to make Zoey get taken? He'd been trying to do everything right. He was working hard on his blog to find missing kids—and with his help, more than a dozen lost kids had been brought home safely. He was also doing everything in his power to be the best dad and fiancé he could be.

Alex wasn't smoking or drinking. He wasn't running with the wrong crowd. Heck, he went to bed at a reasonable hour most nights and even kept his apartment mostly clean so that Zoey and Ariana would actually want to come over.

He racked his mind, trying to think of anything he'd done to make this happen, to piss off some invisible force that made Alex pay for his wrongs in the worst way imaginable.

Nothing. This lifelong screw-up had turned his life around. He was doing good for others and improving the world around him.

Maybe that was part of the problem. Perhaps it was time for some vigilante justice.

STRUGGLE

Zoey fought against the ropes. They burned and had dug into her skin to the point of cutting into it. She didn't care. The only thing that mattered was getting out. Even if it meant running through a neighborhood, cold in only a camisole and ripped pants.

Her captor might think that would be enough to keep her inside, but that was where he was wrong. Dead wrong. She would do whatever it would take to get out of here and back to her family.

Beads of sweat broke out onto her face and dripped down into her eyes. There was nothing she could do but ignore it. It stung, but she didn't care.

She grunted and groaned, fighting against the ropes all the more. One of them might come loose. She wouldn't know if she didn't try.

As much as she struggled, the chair didn't budge. The ropes didn't feel any looser, either. Not yet. Zoey didn't even care how much she hurt herself fighting against the ties, not as long as it would lead to her getting free.

She would fight until she could get out of the gross little house with Ava.

Step, step, step.

Zoey froze.

The gunman was coming back.

Her heart raced. Was he coming to finish his job? He hadn't been able to shoot her at the school.

Step, step.

Zoey's mouth dried. She tried to swallow. Her hair stuck to her face, and a drop of sweat dripped from her forehead, barely missing her eye. She struggled to breathe normally.

He rounded the corner and stopped. "Having fun? Looks like you've been busy."

She glared at him, unable to respond due to the duct tape and gag.

He laughed. "Oh, that's right. You can't answer me."

Zoey struggled more, trying to yell at him even though it came out as nothing more than muffled noises.

"Gotta give you points for trying."

She knitted her brows together.

He walked near her, kicking up dust, but instead of coming over, he went to a counter that connected to a kitchen. From Zoey's angle, it looked just as disgusting as the room she was in. He moved things around, throwing more dust into the air, and then turned around with a sub sandwich and bit into it.

Her stomach rumbled. It had been so long since she'd last eaten. Maybe more than a day at this point. There wasn't any natural light coming into the room, so it was hard to tell.

"Hungry?" He laughed, then took a more dramatic bite.

She struggled all the more against the ties.

"Having fun?"

Zoey wanted to ask if that was his favorite saying. Or maybe he was too stupid to think of something more original. That could be why he needed to carry guns—to make himself feel important.

He took his sweet time eating the sandwich as dramatically as possible, even going so far as to lick his lips and waggle his brows at her.

She couldn't take her attention off the food. Her mouth watered and her stomach continued to growl. Zoey hated how weak the hunger made her—she would do just about anything for even one bite.

Finally, the pig finished it and wiped his hands on his pants. His mouth formed a slow smile, and he looked her over slowly.

"Are you hungry?" he asked.

Zoey narrowed her eyes. What a stupid question. Even if she had eaten before stopping off at the school, she'd be famished by now. He was just taunting her.

"Not going to answer me?" He laughed again.

The sound grated on her last remaining nerve.

"Well, go ahead and keep struggling. It's not going to do you any good. I know how to tie knots you couldn't get through even if you had two free hands."

She continued glaring at him. It was all she had.

"I'll just wait until your attitude improves. Then we can talk about removing the tape and giving you something to eat or drink."

Zoey froze. He was actually going to feed her? Or was he lying to get her to be more cooperative?

"Got your attention, did I? Well, I'm going to leave you to fix your attitude. You'll be a lot better off doing that than trying to break out of the ropes." He sneered at her before storming away.

She waited to see if he would come back. When she heard a door slam, she went back to struggling against the ropes.

SWEET

Genevieve woke, the sound of a snore so close startling her. Then she remembered Nick had stayed over, and she opened her eyes. He lay, sprawled across the bed, the blankets barely covering his bare stomach.

She drew in a deep breath and studied him, wanting to hold onto the image. The night before had been incredible. More than that. It had beat all her daydreams by leaps and bounds. She closed her eyes and relived every moment.

When Genevieve opened her eyes, Nick rolled over toward her. Her breath caught, eager to tell him good morning, and maybe even pick up where they'd left off the night before.

But his eyes remained closed and he let out another little snore. She studied his muscular arms and frame, wanting to run her arms over every inch again. To kiss him all over.

She sighed, hardly able to believe he was actually there. That the night before had happened. But it had.

And the reality was that after he woke, he'd want to get back to the station because his daughter was missing. That had been the reason he'd come over in the first place.

This wasn't a vacation. It was his nightmare, and she'd just given him a distraction. Though hopefully it was much more than that. There was no denying the tension between them that neither had acted on for so long. That was part of what had made last night so magical.

Genevieve rolled to her other side and snuggled next to him, taking in the feel of him being so close. To her surprise, he wrapped an arm around and mumbled something incoherent.

Had he woken? Nick didn't say anything else. He must have mumbled something in his sleep.

She threaded her fingers through his and took a deep breath, enjoying the moment.

Once he woke, they'd both have to make their way to the station. It was her day off, but with the shootout and the bomb, it was all hands on deck. Day off or not, she had to be there.

Though it was possible the feds might come in and offer their support, she would insist on helping. She'd meant it when she told Nick she'd do anything to help find Ava.

Genevieve closed her eyes and let her mind wander... mostly to the night before.

Then her eyes flew open. What would this mean for their jobs? Everything had happened so fast, they hadn't had time to discuss this. Relationships between members of the force were strictly forbidden. Not that it didn't happen from time to time. She heard rumors and also caught the way some people looked at each other, letting their gazes linger. Touches that were slightly more than just friendly.

Did people see that between her and Nick? Nobody had ever said anything, but then again, they may have and Nick set them straight.

But now what? He couldn't honestly deny anything was between them. That was why she had wanted to change departments before allowing anything to happen.

Too late for that now.

Maybe they could just act like everything was normal. And

perhaps nobody would question Nick. He was the captain. Everyone's boss.

Or that might put him under more scrutiny. There were others who wanted his rank.

Genevieve's stomach tightened. The last thing she ever wanted to do was put his job in jeopardy.

It had been hard to think straight last night. He'd been in so much pain, she could feel it. The look in his eyes had cut her to the core. He had even said he'd needed her.

Maybe she should've offered to let him talk. Console him.

What if she'd taken advantage of him? He'd clearly been at a low point. She'd worn her clingiest dress and gone to the extra effort of styling her hair and fixing her makeup before he came over.

Had she ruined everything? What if he woke and realized his job was now on the line?

Her pulse pounded through her body. What had seemed like the right thing the night before now felt like such a mistake in the morning's light.

Nick's hand twitched in hers. "Genevieve?"

Her heart leaped into her throat. It was the moment of truth. Had she ruined the good thing they'd been keeping under control for so long? Working painfully slowly at building?

She swallowed. "Nick."

He squeezed her hand, then let go and traced her arm.

Heart thundering so loud he had to have been able to hear it, she slowly rolled over.

Nick held her gaze, then smiled.

He smiled?

Relief flooded through her.

He ran the back of his fingers along her cheek. "Last night was..." His voice drifted off.

Her voice caught. Last night was wonderful? A mistake?

Nick pressed his lips on hers.

It sent a thrill through her. He didn't think it was a mistake.

"You're so beautiful, you know that?"

Before she could answer, he kissed her again and drew closer.

Click.

The door.

Tinsley would be up by now.

Dread ran through Genevieve. She sat up and turned toward the door.

Sure enough, the girl stood in the doorway.

"Tinsley." Genevieve's mind raced. "I'll get you some breakfast in a minute, okay?"

She just stared at the two of them, wide-eyed.

Nick swore.

Genevieve's heart dropped and shattered. "Go get dressed, okay, honey?"

Tinsley stepped into the hall and disappeared from sight.

Nick swore again, but this time, jumped from the bed and pulled on his clothes.

"Nick—"

"I've got to go."

"She's not going to say anything."

He just stared at her as he pulled on his socks.

"Neither will I. Nothing has to change." Her pulse raced through her body.

Nick didn't respond.

"Tinsley doesn't talk to anyone but me. Well, and her therapist, who can't break client privilege."

"That can't last forever. I have to go. I need to get to the station."

"Can I get you something? Breakfast?"

He shook his head. "I have to get out of here before she comes out of her room."

"I'll explain—"

Without a word, he fled.

MISTAKE

Bile rose in Nick's mouth as he pulled into his parking spot at home.

What had he done?

In a moment of weakness he'd thrown caution to the wind and put his career on the line. He'd pulled Genevieve—Foster—under his wing because he'd seen her potential. It wasn't because she was gorgeous, but who would believe him? The young officer was hot. They'd see Nick as a dirty old man compared to her.

A predator. Someone not fit for being the police captain.

He raced into his apartment to wash off the smell of her perfume. The aroma brought back a wave of memories.

Memories that could kill his career.

What had he been thinking? Not only had he put his job at risk, but he'd gone and given way to passion while his daughter was missing? What kind of sick piece of crap was he?

Ava was probably out there somewhere, cold and scared, and he'd been in the throes of passion.

He was lower than low. Pond scum ranked higher than him.

Not only that, but he'd also put Genevieve's—Foster's—job at risk, too. And given her false hope at a relationship that they couldn't have. Not now. Not until they worked at different precincts and Ava was home, safe and sound.

Nick hurried to get ready, making extra sure he'd gotten rid of any traces of the perfume.

His head also pounded. He poured himself some cereal, then downed it as fast as he could before making coffee. It wasn't enough to get rid of the effects of too many beers last night. He poured an energy drink into the coffee. That would have to do.

He popped a few ibuprofen into his mouth, then headed out the door.

The headache dulled but didn't go away completely as he drove to the station.

As soon as he opened the door, the buzz in the air reminded him of the massive case. One he couldn't be on because he was too close.

Maybe what he needed was to find a new precinct to work at. One in a town where he knew nobody. Then he could work every case that came his way. Plus, then he and Foster could give a relationship an actual try. Now things were just going to be weird between them.

He was stuck between a rock and a hard place. If he just quit partnering with her, people would take notice. But if he continued partnering with her, they would notice something between them. It didn't matter if neither of them—or Tinsley—never said a word, others would pick up on the nonverbal cues. Those would scream louder than any words. But with his luck, the girl would choose talking about what she saw as her first words to the therapist. The police-sanctioned therapist.

"You okay, Captain?"

Nick turned to Garcia. "My daughter's missing. How do you think I'm doing?"

"Right. If you need to take a leave of absence, nobody would blame you."

Nick clenched his fists. "I can handle my job!"

Garcia nodded. "Okay. Well, there was a bank holdup earlier. Paperwork's on your desk."

He gritted his teeth. "I'm on it."

Everything seemed to spin around Nick as he stumbled toward his office. He picked up his feet and walked slower, taking care to look as in control of himself as possible.

Before he reached the office, he noticed some officers flipping through the sketches of the gunman.

"Can I see those?"

"Sure." Grant handed him the stack.

The first drawing hit him like a punch in the gut.

"Are you okay, Captain?"

Nick's hands shook as he flipped through the pages. With the exception of one drawing, the suspect looked like the same man.

Someone Nick could never forget.

He'd met Dave when he'd flown across the country to see his kids. Corrine had been sure the two men met during Nick's quick visit.

"Sir?" Grant asked.

Without a word, Nick snapped a picture of the drawing on top. Then he handed it back to Grant and took a picture of the next one and the next, only leaving out the one that wasn't Dave.

"What's going on?" Grant's eyes were wide with both confusion and hope. "Do you recognize him?"

"I know exactly who he is, though he should be across the country."

"Who is it?"

"Dave Cooper. I'm going to drag his ex-girlfriend over here myself for questioning."

The three officers exchanged glances. Grant cleared his throat. "You're not supposed to be involved, Captain. We should—"

Nick glared at him. "Not involved? Not involved? I couldn't *be* more involved! My daughter is missing and my ex-wife's boyfriend is the gunman!"

Everything took on a red hue.

"Corrine's his girlfriend?" Grant exclaimed.

Nick clenched his fists and breathed heavily. "That's right."

Grant called over Garcia and explained the situation.

Nick stormed to his office and slammed the door, his mind racing. Dave was behind all this?

He had Ava. Nick was as certain of that as he was of his own name. That was why she was missing. He'd taken her.

But why? What was he going to do to her? Did he have his sick son there to finish what he'd started on Halloween?

He picked up a stack of papers from his desk and chucked them across the office. They flew out in all directions, covering the floor.

The door creaked as it opened behind him.

Nick spun around to see Garcia glancing around. "Hey, Nick."

"What do you want?"

"Maybe you should take the day off. What do you think?"

"Do you think I'm too unstable to handle my job?"

Garcia glanced around at the mess. "I think emotions are running high. A break would probably be a good thing. Maybe even a temporary leave of absence. Everyone would understand."

"Would they?"

He nodded slowly. "Definitely. Your daughter is missing. Now isn't the time to be in here."

Nick glared at him. "You don't think I'm capable."

"I think you need to focus on your personal life. Take care of your family. Your other two kids need you now more than ever."

"Fine. I'll go." He pushed past Garcia and stormed out of the station. If he was going to be off-duty, then he would deal with Corrine his own way.

EMERGENCY

Alex rolled over and pulled the pillow over his head. It took him a minute to realize his phone was ringing.

Maybe someone had found Zoey. Or at least had heard something helpful.

He bolted upright and answered the phone without looking at the screen.

"Alex!" It was his dad. "We—"

"Dad! Did they find Zoey?"

"No, but Macy's in labor."

"Already? Isn't she early?"

"Not by much. Can you take her to the hospital?"

"*Take* her?" Alex exclaimed.

"Mom and I have been exposed to the flu, so we don't want to be around her or the baby until we have a medical mask we can wear. We'll have to meet you guys there. Can you take her? I know you're busy trying to help with Zoey, but this is an emergency, too."

"What about Luke?"

"He's at work, and that's in the opposite direction."

"What about an ambulance? They'd be more helpful than me."

Dad sighed. "Macy really wants to try a home birth."

"Then why was she going to the hospital?"

"Because she and Luke couldn't agree. Looks like she's getting her way."

"Seriously?" Alex groaned.

"Yeah. She said she was planning on going natural at the hospital, anyway. You can call them if you need to once you're there. She'll be mad, but she'll get over it. You'll go, right?"

"Of course. I'll be right over."

"Thanks, Alex."

"Sure. Tell her I'll be there." He ended the call and scrambled out of bed, his mind racing. It sucked that Zoey wasn't here for this. She and Macy had all kinds of plans for Zoey being there as the birthing partner or coach or something—now he wished he'd paid more attention. That was probably his job with Zoey gone.

Alex pulled on some clothes and ran a comb through his hair. That would have to be good enough. He threw on a Seahawks cap for good measure, then headed out the door.

It took three tries to lock the deadbolt because his hands were shaking. Then he raced to the car, taking deep breaths. He jumped in and squealed the tires as he pulled out of the spot.

"Calm down," he told himself. "There's plenty of time. Labor can take hours, even more than a day—especially for a first baby."

That *was* true, wasn't it?

His mind went back to the warm summer day Zoey had gone into labor. Macy's water probably broke and the contractions had just gotten intense.

They had plenty of time. He hoped.

Traffic seemed worse than normal, and he also managed to get every red light on the way to Macy and Luke's house. Every single one.

He finally pulled into their neighborhood. The house looked perfectly normal from the outside. Unlike the chaos he imagined inside.

Once parked in the driveway, he flew out of the car. He didn't bother knocking, and as expected, the door was unlocked.

"Macy!"

"In here!" Her voice came from the direction of the bedroom.

Alex ran over. "Where are your bags?"

His sister was pacing the room with both hands on her back and breathing heavily.

"Where are the bags?"

She stopped pacing and turned to him. "I don't think I'm going to make it."

"You think you're going to die?" Alex exclaimed.

Macy shook her head and took some more deep breaths. "No, Alex. I think the baby's going to come before we get there."

He just stared at her for a moment, then shook his head. "You'll make it."

"The contractions are too close together." She went back to pacing and breathing heavily.

"We have to try! Come on."

"Alex, trust me on this. There isn't time." Macy's eyes widened and she clutched her stomach before screaming.

His stomach twisted in knots and his mind went back to Ariana's birth. Everything was a blur in his mind, especially with his sister yelling.

He raced over, put his arms around her, and guided her to the bed. Instead of sitting, Macy put her hands on it and squatted.

"What are you doing? You need to lay down!"

She shook her head and squeezed the covers. "This is more... natural than... laying."

"So the baby can land on its head? If we're going to do this here, you need to lay down, okay? What do you want—the bed or the couch?"

Macy rested her head on the covers and yelled again.

"What am I supposed to do?" He vaguely recalled hearing

something about towels and boiling water. For what, he had no idea. "I'll call Luke!"

His sister screamed again.

Alex rubbed her back, feeling like an idiot. He needed to *do* something. Get on the ground to catch the baby?

Macy stopped yelling and went back to pacing.

"I really think you're supposed to be on the bed."

She shook her head and wiped sweat from her brow. "Walking is better."

"Then why did the hospital have Zoey on the bed?"

Macy took several deep breaths. "When have you ever known hospitals to go the natural route?"

"I have no idea, but I can't imagine the baby being born on the floor is a good idea."

"That's not how it works. Someone's supposed to be there to guide the baby out."

"I'm calling Luke and our parents. They're all heading to the hospital." And any one of them could catch the baby. No way did Alex want that kind of responsibility. He was just supposed to drive her to the hospital! "Are you going to be okay?"

"I'm fine until the next wave hits."

Alex whipped out his phone and called his brother-in-law, who didn't answer. "He must be driving. I'll text him."

If Macy heard, she didn't respond.

Next, Alex called his dad.

"Are you at the hospital?" he answered.

"That fast? No, Macy says the baby's almost here and there isn't enough time."

"What?"

"That's what I said."

Macy cried out again.

"Those *are* close! When are you going to get here, Dad?"

"We're going to have to turn around and buy some masks at the store."

"Do you know where Luke is?"

"Stuck on the freeway. There's a bad accident that has traffic stopped. He's nowhere near an exit."

Alex tugged on his hair. "Of course he's not. Hurry, okay?"

"We'll do our best. Do you need us to get anything at the store?"

"I'll ask Macy." Alex covered the phone and asked his sister, who just waved him off and continued pacing. "She's distracted, Dad. What am I supposed to do?"

"Put some towels on the bed and get her to sit on them."

"That'll be easier said than done."

"Huh?"

"Never mind. I'll see you when you get here." Alex ended the call and brought over every towel from the linen closet and spread them on the bed. "Macy, come on over here."

She turned and started to say something, but then clutched her stomach again and screamed.

He ran over and guided her to the bed. Thankfully, she crawled on top of the towels without complaint.

Once she quieted, she turned to Alex. "You're going to have to deliver my baby."

Everything other than his sister disappeared from his vision.

"Alex?"

"Um, okay. Sure. What am I supposed to do?"

"Start by washing your hands."

"Right." Alex headed for the bathroom and texted Luke, not that it sounded like he'd be there in time.

FIGHT

Nick pounded on Corrine's door.

The door flung open and his ex-wife glared at him. "What's wrong with you?"

He stormed inside, pushing past her. "I should ask you the same thing."

"What are you talking about?" she demanded.

Nick clenched his fists and jutted his jaw. "Our daughter."

"What?"

"This is all your fault!"

"Would you keep your voice down? The kids are both sleeping. I couldn't get them to calm down until after midnight."

He stepped closer. "And whose fault is that?"

"Why don't you tell me?"

"Yours!"

"Nick, would you calm down and start making some sense?"

"Sure thing." He pulled out his phone and found the first picture of the sketches. "How about this?"

Corrine glanced at the screen, then color drained from her face. "What's that?"

"A picture of Dave, wouldn't you say?"

"But I mean, what's it for? Who drew that? And why?"

Nick swiped over to the next sketch of her ex-boyfriend.

Corrine's mouth dropped, then she sat down. She knew without Nick having to say a word.

But that wasn't going to stop him. He swiped over to the next one. "These are what people say the school shooter looks like. He bears a striking resemblance to your stewardess boyfriend, doesn't he?"

For once in her life, Corrine appeared to be speechless.

"And Ava's missing. That must be a coincidence, don't you think? Or wait. Is it? His perverted son is probably upset about not being able to finish what he started. Think Dave took her so his creepy kid can get his way with her?"

"Can... can I see those again?"

Nick handed her the phone.

She swiped the screen, slumping further down the chair each time. "I think I'm going to be sick."

Corrine shoved the phone in Nick's palm, then bolted out of the room. Sounds of her retching came from down the hallway.

At least that indicated his ex wasn't involved in the whole ordeal.

Nick paced the living room, a slight wave of nostalgia running through him. Almost all the furniture had been in their home. They'd picked it out together before she decided to rip their family apart.

Most everything in Nick's apartment had been handed down from friends and family or had been garage sale purchases. He'd been lucky to keep his prize Mustang the way her lawyer had played dirty, even managing to get the judge to allow her to move across the country with the kids—where she would meet Dave.

Nick had half a mind to find both the attorney and judge and inform them of their parts in the school shooting.

Corrine stumbled back into the living room. "You're telling the truth? Dave is actually the gunman?"

"According to the witnesses."

She put her palms over her face and mumbled something he couldn't understand. A minute later, she looked up at him. "Do you have any leads on where he is?"

"No. Do you have any idea?"

She shook her head. "I didn't even know he was in the area. We broke up, and I made it clear we were through. No more contact."

"Looks like he listens as well as his kid." Nick walked around the room, studying pictures of the kids—pictures he hadn't seen in a long time. "I have to ask, did you have anything to do with this?"

Corrine actually looked hurt. "Of course not! Do you think I'd put my daughter at risk?"

"She *was* sexually assaulted on your watch."

"Don't be so dramatic, Nick. Mason felt her up, then Ava got away. Boys did worse stuff than that at school when we were kids. Teachers said boys would be boys. You remember how it was."

Nick clenched his jaw. "Unwanted fondling is sexual assault. Don't try to play it down. Your boyfriend's son assaulted our daughter."

Corrine sat and looked at her hands.

He almost felt sorry for her. Almost.

Silence hung in the air between them until she glanced back up at him. "Why are you here and not at work? Shouldn't you be trying to solve this rather than making me feel bad?"

He laughed bitterly.

"What?"

"You're unbelievable."

"Why?"

"Your whole argument against me has always been that I spend too much time at work. I'm married to my job, you said. The kids barely recognize me. I work and sleep, and nothing else. Now you're upset that I'm not there."

"It's not like that."

"What is it like, then?" He stared her down.

"Our daughter is missing! You're wasting your time being here when you should be hunting Dave down."

"You do realize that I can't be on the case, don't you? The fact that Ava's missing prevents me. In fact, I've agreed to take a leave of absence."

"Now, of all times?" She jumped up. "You need to be working now more than ever!"

Nick stormed toward the door, then turned back and glared at her. "If you think of anything that could help, call the station. I'll be here to pick up the kids on Friday, just like usual." He flung open the door, and just as he did, a police cruiser pulled up in front of the house. "Looks like you won't have to call, after all."

Her face paled even more. "I'm not a suspect, am I?"

"I wouldn't know. I'm not on the case. But you might want to call your lawyer. He's good at getting you what you think you deserve."

Corrine's mouth dropped. "Nick, don't go."

"Funny. I remember saying the same thing to you when you moved my kids across the country from me." He stepped outside and slammed the door.

TIME

Alex wiped Macy's forehead. "You're doing great."
She continued her rhythmic breathing and didn't look
at him.

He brought the glass of water to her mouth and pushed the
straw to her lips. She drank a little.

"Can I get you anything else?"

Macy shook her head, taking deep breaths.

"Some more ibuprofen?"

"No. It's not helping! And besides, I'm a little pissed at you for
talking me into that after I told you I wanted this to be natural."

"I'm fine with that. Do you want another—?"

"Where's Luke?" She pushed the glass away and gasped for air.

Alex set it on the nightstand. "Stuck in traffic. His last text said
he finally got off the freeway but the side streets are stopped."

"He didn't text and drive, did he?" She drew in deep breaths.

"I'm sure he didn't."

"Where's Zoey?" she demanded.

Alex jumped up to his feet. "I need to get you fresh water."

She glared at him and wiped sweat from her forehead. "Why
do you keep changing the subject when I bring her up?"

"I'm not." His tone gave away his lie.

"You're a horrible liar!" She squeezed her pillow.

He was out of practice since turning his life around. "I—"

Macy yelled again and closed her eyes, clutching her stomach.

Alex grabbed her hand, and she squeezed so hard he expected to feel bones crunching.

As soon as she stopped, she gasped for air and met Alex's gaze. She released a string of profanities. "This one has to be it! You're going to have to help the baby out!"

His stomach tightened. In between Macy's contractions, he'd looked up directions online. "Can't you just wait a little longer? Luke's almost here."

She looked at him like he was crazy. His suggestion was, but if there was any chance she *could* hold off, he wanted to throw that out there.

"You can do this, Alex!" Macy hiked up her oversized shirt to her waist.

He immediately turned the other way.

"Come on! The next one might be it!" She screamed, more sweat forming around her hairline.

"How do you know?" Alex exclaimed, still looking away.

"I can just tell! Grow up. This isn't anything you've never seen before!"

"You're my *sister!* I've never seen that before."

"Stop being a baby! I need you to do this!"

He took a deep breath. "Okay. You're right." Suddenly, a wave of pride washed through him. He *wanted* to do this, to help out Macy and his little niece or nephew.

Alex climbed on the bed and focused on Macy's face.

She gasped for air, then gave him a little smile. "Thank you. You don't know what this means to me."

"I'm happy to help. Really."

Macy took a deep breath. "Where's Zoey?"

Not this again. The last thing Macy needed right now was to worry about her best friend. She could find out later.

"Alex?" She glared at him.

"She really wants to be here. I swear. More than anything. She just, uh—"

Macy yelled out and closed her eyes.

Relief washed through Alex, but only for a moment. Until he realized the baby was going to come this time—if his sister was right. And it was his job to get it out.

She screamed louder, and it seemed longer, than the times before.

He peeked down at the birthing site. Sure enough, the top of a head was already showing. Alex's pulse raced through his body. He couldn't remember a thing he'd read.

Why had he agreed to this? And why wasn't anyone else here? How had it ended up being him? What if he messed this up? There were two lives in his hands.

Something in the living room caught his attention. Luke was throwing off his coat and removing his shoes.

"We're in here!" Alex called, then felt stupid. Of course they were in there. The entire neighborhood could probably hear Macy.

Luke raced in. "Just let me wash my hands." He kissed Macy's cheek. "I'm here, babe."

Alex stayed in position until Luke returned from the bathroom. His heart pounded and his knees nearly gave out as he stumbled into the living room.

In the bedroom, he heard Luke coaching and encouraging Macy. He, at least, sounded like he knew what he was doing. It was almost like they had planned it this way.

Alex crashed on the couch and took deep breaths of his own. A few minutes later, his parents burst inside, both wearing yellow masks over their mouths and noses.

Macy's cries stopped, then a tiny cry began.

"It's a boy!" Luke called out.

Alex exchanged excited glances with his parents before they all made their way to the bedroom.

Macy was fully covered, and both she and Luke held the tiny crying baby.

His nephew. Alex was an uncle!

Alex ran over and put his arm around Macy, then embraced Luke. "Congratulations, you guys! What's his name?"

The new parents exchanged a glance. Macy turned to Alex. "We're stuck between two. We'll let you all know as soon as we decide."

Alex stared proudly at the little guy. "Welcome to the world."

CONFLICTED

Genevieve peeked into Nick's office after a full minute of knocking without a response. Papers lay strewn all over, but Nick wasn't there.

Maybe he'd been called out somewhere since everyone else was busy with the shooting and two missing persons.

She stepped inside, picked up the loose papers, and stacked them on his desk before looking around for any sign of where he may have gone.

There was none. Not that she should've expected anything.

Genevieve went over to Detective Anderson's desk. "Have you seen the captain?"

"He's taking a leave of absence."

She gave him a double-take. "Since when?"

It had barely been two hours since she last saw him, and he hadn't said anything to her. But then again, he'd also been upset and distracted.

Her stomach tightened. Was he avoiding her? She swallowed and tried to hide her worry. "Do you know why?"

"He's too upset over his missing daughter." The detective's tone held a "duh" to it.

Her face flamed. "Right, of course. Any new developments?"

"I heard we have the name of a potential suspect, but I don't know any details. I'm looking some stuff up for the feds."

"Thanks." Genevieve spun around and fled to her desk before she could make a bigger fool of herself. She had to pull herself together. The last thing either she or Nick needed was for anyone to figure out what had happened between them the night before.

She felt like she was wearing a flashing neon sign, like everyone could sense what they'd done. Of course that was ridiculous, but the feeling wouldn't go away.

Once she was sure nobody was looking, she sent him a quick text asking if he was okay, and then she went to work. There was enough to do to keep her busy for a week without even needing to leave her desk. That was just as well. She was in no state of mind to be out dealing with the public.

Genevieve pushed everything from her mind and focused on the task at hand. Before she knew it, a couple hours had flown by. Still no text back from Nick.

Her stomach twisted. Not that they usually spent much time texting back and forth. They weren't in a relationship. It was just that with the night before and the way he'd left, she needed to know that everything was okay. That they hadn't ruined the good thing they'd had going.

She felt like kicking herself for inviting him over. For wearing that dress and basically inviting him to kiss her and forget about his problems for a while. All she'd done was push him away. Destroyed any chance they had at a real relationship—the one thing she really wanted.

Focus!

Genevieve turned back to the paperwork and her computer and chastised herself for worrying about what Nick thought of her. He was concerned about one thing, and that was finding his daughter. It was far more important than anything else.

Officer Chang stopped at her desk and leaned against it. "A

bunch of us are heading over to that new Indian restaurant. Want to join us?"

"Yeah. Meet you there."

"You can ride with me. I have room." He ran his fingers through his hair slowly and drew his eyebrows together. "Save on gas, and all that."

"Okay, sure." She grabbed her purse and followed him. At least hanging out with some of the other officers for a while might help to get her mind off everything.

Except it didn't. Conversation didn't drift away from the shooting or the two missing people. Theories flew around the table like gnats at a summer barbecue. Everyone was excited that a suspect had been named based off the police sketches.

Genevieve wiped her mouth with a napkin. "I didn't hear about that. Who did they name?"

Chang held her gaze for a moment. "Some guy the captain's ex was seeing. He's the one who identified him. Said he was a hundred percent sure."

The news felt like a slap to the face. "And he took his leave of absence after that?"

Grant nodded and leaned over the table. "He threw quite the fit. Can't really blame the guy, though. If someone my ex dated did that and took my kid, I'd be seeing red myself."

Genevieve nearly dropped her napkin. "Sounds like he really needed to step away from the case."

Chang snorted. "My money's on him not staying away from the case."

She sat taller and stared him down. "He's as professional as they come. If he says he's taking time off, that's what he's doing."

He held her gaze. "You'd know."

"What's that supposed to mean?"

All other conversation at their table grew quiet.

Chang leaned back in his chair. "Just saying you two work together a lot. That's all."

Her face warmed, and she hoped it didn't turn pink. She pressed her palms on the table. "It sounds like you're saying more than that."

"Do I have reason?"

"If you want to accuse me of something, why don't you just say it?"

A few people around the table mumbled to each other.

Chang fixed his collar and continued holding her gaze. "Just making an observation. Nothing more."

Her pulse raced through her body. There was so much she wanted to say, but doing so would only make her and Nick look guilty. "All right then, let's talk about something else."

"Fine by me." His brows knit together as he continued staring at her, then he finally turned his attention to one of the others.

She sipped her drink, trying to calm herself. Why had she agreed to ride with Chang?

SHOCK

Zoey leaned back in the chair. Her muscles ached, her head pounded, and her stomach hadn't stopped growling. All of that was starting to pale in comparison to the rope burns on her ankles and wrists.

She drew in several deep breaths through her nose and shook her head to keep sweat from dripping into her eyes.

Trying to get out of the ties was turning into a futile cause. She was probably giving herself marks that would never go away—assuming she got away. There was no telling what the captor was going to do with her.

Why bring her all the way to wherever they were? The car ride had seemed to go on for hours. Though it likely seemed longer due to being tied up on the floor underneath a blanket. It was like he purposefully ran over every bump in the road.

The longer Zoey sat still, the colder she became, until she started shivering. If she didn't keep fighting against the ropes, would she get so cold she'd die? Was that the plan? Or would starvation get to her first?

Maybe *that* was his plan. He hadn't been able to kill her back at the school, so he'd brought her here to die. It was a long way to drive just for that, especially when all he'd had to do was reload one of his guns.

And what about Ava? Where was she? He'd been dragging her around like he had some kind of plan for her.

Zoey shivered, and it made all of her pain all the worse. Even with as miserable as she felt, her eyelids grew heavy. It was tempting to give in, but could she even sleep tied sitting upright? She certainly wouldn't stay warm—she would only grow colder wearing just a camisole and ripped pants.

If only she could get over to the kitchen and rummage through it to find something to eat. She would take anything at this point.

She had to keep fighting. Sleep would have to wait. The exhaustion would have to move over, because she didn't have any other choice. Getting back to Ariana and Alex wasn't optional. It would happen.

Zoey went back to struggling against the ties. They dug into her already-sore skin. Tears stung her eyes, but she blinked them away and kept struggling. She would get free or die trying.

Creak!

She froze. Was he coming back?

Scrape-scrape.

Her throat closed up and she struggled to breathe. It was twice as hard without the use of her mouth. She wanted to scream at the top of her lungs. But she had to save her energy for running.

If she ever got the chance.

Crash!

Zoey struggled against the ties all the harder. She didn't want to find out what was going on.

Creak-creak.

A door cracked open. It was one Zoey had thought was a closet.

The door opened farther, but nobody came out.

Her eyes widened. She struggled all the more. If she could've run and hid somewhere, she would have. Instead, she was in the middle of the room, exposed to whatever monster was about to come out for her. Possibly something far worse than the gunman.

The door moved even more, now halfway open. Due to the dim light and shadows, Zoey couldn't see anything—anyone. Was it another captive like her? Or someone worse than her captor?

Crash! Thud!

A plume of dust rose from the ground. It took Zoey a moment to realize someone had fallen to the floor from behind the door.

She simultaneously wanted to scream and run. She could do neither.

The person didn't move for a moment, but then rose.

It was Ava. She was still fully clothed, thank God. As she struggled to stand, she looked around the room, then finally her gaze landed on Zoey.

Her mouth dropped. "Miss Carter?"

Zoey struggled against the ties and tried to call out to the girl.

"Why does Dave have you? Have you seen my brother or sister?" Ava asked.

Zoey shook her head and continued whining—the only sound she could make with any real volume.

Ava wobbled toward her. "I need to get the keys to the cuffs on my ankles. Then I'll get you untied. We have to run. I think Dave left, but who knows how long he'll be gone?"

Zoey moved back and forth, and tried to shout, for all the good that did. What they needed was for Ava to free her, then they could both look for the key, and find some food while they were at it.

The girl continued talking, but Zoey couldn't focus. She just needed to get out of the chair. The sooner the better.

Once Ava finally made it to Zoey, she knelt down and pulled on the rope on Zoey's right wrist. It seemed to take forever, but her arm finally fell free.

Zoey reached for the duct tape and yanked it from her mouth, then she pulled out the gag. She gasped in as much air as she could.

Ava freed her other hand.

"Thank you!" Zoey stared at her red rope-burned wrists. They looked a lot better than they felt. She'd expected to see bloody flesh hanging from her bones.

"We've got to get out of here!" Ava moved to Zoey's left foot. "Dave's crazy, and he might not be alone."

"I gathered as much." Zoey bent over and reached for her other leg.

A door slammed shut somewhere not far away.

Zoey and Ava exchanged a worried glance.

"Go back!" Zoey gestured toward the door Ava had come out of. "I'll look for that key. Don't let him know we're trying to escape. That we're working together. Hurry!"

Ava nodded, then scrambled on all fours back to the room, moving much faster than she had before.

Just after she closed the door behind her, Dave appeared around the corner.

Zoey pulled her arms back against the chair as they'd been before. Hopefully, Dave wouldn't notice the ropes on the floor or the missing duct tape from her mouth.

CONVINCE

Alex called Nick. Again. It went to voicemail as it had the last fifty or so times. At least it felt like fifty attempts.

Luke came out of the bedroom and brushed some hair from his eyes. He plopped down next to Alex on the couch.

"How're Macy and the baby?"

"Both are sleeping. The doctor wants me to bring her to the hospital, but she just wants to rest first. Says she won't be able to sleep at all once there. I'm sure she's right."

Alex thought back to his recent stay at one. "True. They never seem to give you ten minutes to yourself. Do you need anything?"

Luke shook his head. "You've got enough on your plate. Thanks for coming over. We really didn't think Macy would go into labor so soon, or that it would happen so fast."

"She's my sister. I'd do anything for her."

"Still, I appreciate it. At least you were here when I couldn't be."

Silence rested between them until Alex spoke. "How long do you think you'll be able to keep the news about Zoey from her? She was so persistent earlier. The baby crowning was the only thing that finally distracted her."

Luke closed his eyes. "That sounds like Macy."

"She's going to want to know why her best friend isn't here to support her."

"I know." Luke opened his eyes. "I'll figure something out. If she really won't relent, I'll give her part of the story. Make it sound not so bad. She'll be mad at me later, but it's worth it for her to not be stressed right now."

"You can blame it on me. Tell her I threatened to hit you."

Luke cracked a small smile. "Just find Zoey so Macy never has to know anything was ever wrong."

"That's my plan." Alex checked his phone. Still no calls or texts from his friend. "Well, if you're fine and they're sleeping, I'm going to take off."

Luke nodded. "Thanks again for everything."

"Don't mention it." Alex shook his hand. "Congrats again. I'll call or stop by later."

"Sounds good. Let me know if you hear anything about Zoey."

Alex nodded, then made his way outside. His car was parked diagonally across the driveway, leaving no room for anyone else. Luke's car was next to the sidewalk in front of the house.

No time to worry about that. Alex climbed in and texted Nick to let him know he was going to his office and then his house to find him.

Just as Alex was pulling out of the driveway, his phone rang. He accepted the call and put it on speaker. "Took you long enough."

"I'm busy, Alex." Nick sounded out of breath.

"What's going on? Do you know where they are?"

"No. That's why I'm so busy, but I do know who has them."

Alex pulled over. "What? For real?"

"Yeah. All the sketches except yours were of Dave."

"Dave? Dave, who?"

"Corrine's boyfriend."

"*That* Dave? What's he doing here?"

"Shooting up a school and holding my daughter."

Alex squeezed the steering wheel. "Why does he have Zoey?"

There was a brief silence before Nick replied. "That's anyone's guess."

"It sounds like you have an idea."

"He's a sick bastard, what can I say?"

Alex thought back to what Dave's son did to Ava. "You mean like his kid? You think he wants to... to..." He couldn't bring himself to say it. "To Zoey?"

"Maybe. I don't know. If I did, he'd have a bullet through his brain already."

Alex's stomach lurched. "Where are they? Do you have *any* idea?"

"That's what I'm trying to figure out."

"Can't you do that faster?"

"No, actually I can't. Especially since I'm not on the case. In fact, I'm not even working. I'm taking a leave of absence."

"What?" Alex exclaimed. "But you can stay on top of everything if you're there."

"I can't think straight. It makes more sense than any other time."

"We have to take this into our own hands, then."

"No, Alex, we can't."

"Nobody cares about this case more than we do! Our skin is in the game like no one else's."

Nick took a deep breath. "I realize that, and that makes us more likely to screw up. I'm not going to do that. My daughter's life is on the line. I'm not going to pull the crap you did when Ariana was gone."

Alex gritted his teeth. "I resent that."

"You ended up under arrest, Alex! You should've let us handle it."

"The charges never stuck. You know that! If I hadn't done everything I did—"

"Alex, I need to go. As much as I don't want to, I need to go

109

back to Corrine's. The officers just left, and I need to find out everything I can from her about Dave."

"See? You're getting involved off the books!"

"The difference is that I'm not doing anything illegal. I'm going to find out what I can from her. I can communicate with her in ways they can't. Then once I find out what I need to, I'll tell the head of the case."

"What am I supposed to do?"

"Do what you do best. Blog about it. You have extensive reach."

"Can I at least post a picture of Dave? Tell about his past?"

"They've already released one of the sketches to the press. They're working on an actual picture. It's public knowledge. Everyone needs to know what he looks like. Yes, post everything you know. I'll talk to you later." The call ended.

Alex fought to breathe normally. The thought of Zoey and Ava with Dave made him sick to his stomach.

He would try it Nick's way—staying within the bounds of the law—but if that didn't work, Alex wouldn't hesitate to do what it took to get Zoey and Ava back safe and sound. As long as he wasn't an officer yet, he was still a normal citizen. He could get away with a lot more, and he would take full advantage of that.

QUESTION

Nick marched up Corrine's walkway and rapped on the door.

She answered, looking both exhausted and annoyed. "What do you want? Your buddies just left."

"I know. That's why I'm here."

Corrine groaned. "You never left?"

"I'm an extremely patient man. Are you going to let me in?"

"You're not going to leave if I say no?"

He shook his head.

"I can call you in for stalking."

Nick arched a brow. "Really? You think that'll work? What evidence do you have?"

She threw her hands in the air. "Fine. Come in. You're going to eventually, so I may as well get this over with."

He walked in past her. "I just want to find Ava. Nothing more."

"That's all I want." She slammed the door. "I don't see how you being here is going to help."

"We're just going to chat. See what we can figure out about where Dave might be."

"Because you don't trust your guys to do a good enough job?"

"Because I think you might be more relaxed talking to me. You'll probably think of things you didn't with the officers here."

Corrine laughed. "Relaxed around you? Are you delusional?"

Nick plunked down on the couch and kicked his feet up onto the coffee table. Just like he'd done thousands of times before on this very furniture. "Not delusional at all."

She folded her arms. "So, we're just going to sit and talk about my ex like old friends?"

"Why not?" He crossed one foot over the other.

"Maybe because we hate each other?"

"Do we? Really?"

They stared each other down before she uncrossed her arms. "I'm going to get something to drink—I need it. Want something?"

"Sure."

"What?"

"Surprise me."

Corrine gave him half an eye roll, then disappeared into the kitchen. Glasses banged around.

Nick looked around the room, studying the pictures of the kids. He didn't have nearly enough of them. The only ones she hadn't taken were the ones on his phone and backed up on the cloud.

Corrine returned with a martini in one hand and a White Russian in the other—Nick's favorite.

Neither said anything as she handed it to him. He sipped it as she sat two cushions over.

"What do you think I'm going to tell you that I didn't tell your brothers in blue?"

He shrugged. "Guess we'll see. You'd have a better idea than I would."

"If you think I'm hiding something from them, you're wrong. I want them to find him as much as anyone. Actually, I'd like them to give me five minutes with him. I'd tear him to shreds for every-thing he's done."

Nick took another sip. "That makes two of us."

She arched a brow. "Are you, the police captain, admitting you'd harm a man if given the chance?"

"We're just shooting the breeze, Corrine. Two friends talking."

Her expression twisted in confusion.

He finished his drink and set the glass on the table.

"You want another one?"

Was she trying to get him drunk so he'd say something stupid? He shook his head. "I'm good. Thanks for the drink."

She nodded and continued working on hers.

"Any ideas where Dave would go?"

"Like I told your guys, I have no clue. As far as I know, he's never been to Washington. If he has ties here, he kept them from me."

Nick nodded. "Has he been temperamental in the past? With you? Anyone else?"

"Are you trying to say I put my kids in danger?"

"I'm just trying to understand the man. The more I know about him, the better the likelihood that I can make an educated guess as to where he might be with our daughter."

"He has no more of a temper than anyone else. In fact, he's usually the most easy-going guy around. Tells a lot of jokes and loves to make people laugh."

"Really?"

"You don't believe me?"

"That hardly sounds like the type of guy who goes on a killing rampage. Or has a kid who is a sexual predator."

"Would you lay off Mason?"

"Why do you always defend him? You should be more worried about our daughter."

"You think I'm not? I moved here, getting her away from them, didn't I? Leave Mason out of this."

"Okay, okay." For now. Something didn't sit right with him

about the way she always defended the kid. It never had. But he'd have to get her talking about other things first.

They sat in silence. It wasn't quite comfortable, but it was closer than they'd been in a long time.

"Kids still sleeping?" Nick finally asked.

Corrine nodded. "They fell asleep really late, even Hanna."

He hated that they had to deal with this. It made it all the more important for him to get what he could out of his ex. "Has Dave ever done anything to hurt any of the kids before?"

"What? No! How could you even ask that?"

He stared at her.

She threw her arms into the air. "I mean, don't you know I'd never allow that?"

"So, all this—coming all the way here, shooting up a school, blowing up part of it, and abducting Ava and Zoey—it's completely out of character for him?"

"Yes! Like I said, he was always easygoing and funny. I can't think of a person who didn't love him."

Nick frowned, trying to put all the pieces together. "People don't usually act so far from their personality. Did you see any signs that he was hiding a temper? Or maybe had a quiet side?"

She was silent for a moment. "Well, at home he liked his solitude. Loved reading and spending time online. Maybe his jokes were covering something else up. I don't know. But I never got the feeling anything was wrong. I mean, if anyone would, it'd be me."

"If you were living with him, yeah."

"I told you, we weren't living together."

"You don't have to keep saying that anymore. You're back here and we have fifty-fifty custody of the kids."

She frowned, obviously believing that if she admitted to living with the psycho, he would go for more than that. Living with him had broken their agreement.

Nick grew impatient. "I need to get going. If you think of

anything, tell me or the officers who were here. He needs to be caught."

"You think I don't know that?" she snapped.

There was the Corrine he knew so well.

He rose. "Just let someone know. All I want is to bring him to justice before anyone else gets hurt."

INTIMIDATION

Ava pressed her ear against the door. Dave was still ranting. It didn't sound like he was hurting Zoey. Just yelling a lot.

She hated when he got like that. It was always behind closed doors. Dave put on a good show of being the funny guy that everyone liked, but it was all a lie. He even hid it from her mom most of the time. But as soon as all the adults were away from him, he turned into a different person. A horrible one. Although, Ava never would have guessed he was capable of killing people.

His yelling had stopped, for now. She pressed her ear to the door in several different places, still not hearing anything.

Ava scooted away and leaned against a wall. She needed to find a way to get the cuffs off. Not only did they dig into her ankles, but they made it impossible to walk, much less fight.

Stupid jerk. She never should've been nice to him. For her mom's sake, she'd tried to hold back her snark and attitudes. If she could go back in time, she'd give him an earful. Actually, if she could just get the handcuffs off her legs, she'd let him have it.

Some things were easier said than done.

She hoped he would leave again. Zoey and she could search for the key. Then they could leave. Get as far away as they could, then get help. Tell the cops where Dave was staying.

Ava imagined a dramatic arrest, then everyone heaping praise on them for surviving to stop a monster. They would be famous. She closed her eyes and let herself get lost in the fantasy. It was all she had to hang onto.

The door next to her flung open and slammed against the wall. She jumped and glanced over.

Dave glared at her. "What are you doing on the floor?"

"Sitting here. What does it look like?"

He hit her across the face. "Don't give me lip. I'm sick of all your attitude."

Ava covered her cheek, where it was already warm and throbbing from the slap. "Attitude? I've always been nice to you."

"You, nice? You're about as sweet as poison."

Her mouth dropped. "At least I don't tell stupid jokes that people only pretend to think are funny."

He slapped her across the other side of her face, then grabbed her arm, squeezing hard, and forced her to stand. "I wouldn't mess with me if I were you."

She cried out. It felt like he was ripping her muscle. "Stop."

"No, *you* stop. I'm the one in charge here. You have to listen to me." He dragged her over to the bed and threw her on it. "Stay here."

Ava glared at him and struggled to sit up. "When are you going to take these cuffs off?"

He grabbed her other arm and squeezed just as hard. "You don't get to ask questions. Stay here."

She blinked back tears, refusing to let him see how easily he was getting to her. "I'm hungry! Bored!"

Dave made a mock-sympathetic expression and managed to apply more pressure on her arm. "Oh, is the poor baby having a hard time functioning without her phone? This'll be good for you, especially if we finally get rid of that chip on your shoulder."

Ava struggled to get free of his grasp, but he dug his fingers deeper. Tears fought all the harder, but she wouldn't let him see them. She spit in his face.

Shock covered his expression for a moment, then he shoved her on her back while swearing at her and wiping his face. "You're going to regret that."

"No, I won't." Ava spit again, though it wasn't much since her mouth was so dry from having gone so long without eating or drinking anything.

He grabbed both her arms and shoved them back underneath her.

Her arms felt like they were going to pop out of the sockets. Sharp pain shot through them like nothing she'd experienced. She bit her tongue to keep from crying out.

"You will learn to obey me! I'll wait as long as it takes." He forced her arms back further, like he was actually trying to pull them from the sockets.

It took all of Ava's strength not to scream.

"Are you ready to cooperate yet?" His nostrils flared and spittle flew from his mouth, spraying onto her face.

Ava gave a slight nod.

"What was that? I couldn't hear you."

She nodded more dramatically.

"I said, I can't *hear* you."

Ava fought to breathe normally. She would agree to just about anything to get him to let go of her arms. "Okay." Her voice came out quiet and pinched.

"Okay, what?"

She fought the threatening tears and squirmed to try to ease the pain in her sockets. "I'll cooperate."

"Good." He let go of her.

Relief washed through her, though the pain didn't fully go away. She shook out her arms and took a deep breath, still fighting the stupid tears. She would *not* let him see her weakness.

Then she noticed her knees were between his legs—right where she could knee him in the balls.

Dave was talking, but Ava couldn't focus. She could knee him and then shove him, but then what? He might pin her down again, harder. Her arms throbbed where he'd squeezed and her shoulders ached horribly. Then there was the matter of the cuffs on her ankles.

Stupid, stupid jerk.

In one quick motion, she hefted both her knees up and nailed him in the crotch as hard as she could. She had one chance, and she wasn't going to waste it.

His eyes widened and he stumbled back for just a moment. Then his eyes fixed on her and his whole face tensed.

Terror ran through Ava. She scrambled to sit up and rolled over to the other side of the bed. It shook as Dave's weight thrust down on it. Ava swung her feet to the floor and scooted as fast as she could.

Dave's fingers wrapped around her arm again. This time, he dug his nails into her skin. He yanked her back and pulled on her hair for an extra grip. "You're really going to regret that."

INTIMIDATION

Heart pounding, Zoey finally loosened the last tie. She kicked her feet and jumped up. She was free!

Somehow, Dave hadn't noticed the tape removed from her mouth when he had been yelling at her. Also, in all his pacing and raving, he hadn't walked behind the chair to notice her hands were now free of those ropes.

As soon as he went into the room where Ava was, Zoey had worked on her last two ties. They'd been tough, but thankfully not impossible, to undo.

In the other room, Ava cried out.

Zoey glanced around for something she could use as a weapon. Anything would work. Unfortunately, none of the junk looked helpful. Even the chair had been secured to the ground. That sicko had thought of everything.

Ava cried out again. Zoey flinched. She ran over to the kitchen, just in case Dave had left a knife lying out. Or anything. Anything would do. She didn't have time to rummage through the drawers and cabinets.

Something crashed against a wall in Ava's room. Zoey bolted out of the kitchen and into the room.

He had the girl pinned to the bed with his back to Zoey.

She had the element of surprise on her side, not that it would do her good for long. Her entire body ached and her head still throbbed. Once he figured out what was going on, he would easily overpower her.

Still, she had to do what she could. Between her and Ava, they might be able to overwhelm him. They had to. There was no other option.

Zoey clenched her fists and prepared to attack. She ran at him and threw all her weight against his back. He stumbled to the side, his arms flailing. She nearly fell on top of Ava, but managed to catch herself and lunge toward Dave again.

He turned to her, his eyes wide.

"Didn't expect to see me, did you?" Zoey balled her fist and punched him in the nose. Blood sprayed out and he reached for it.

Ava sat up, sniffling and rubbing her arm. Her face was tear-stained and her eyes puffy. A red handprint colored one cheek.

Zoey turned back to Dave and flung herself at him again, this time knocking him off the bed. He landed with a crash and dust flew into the air.

She rolled off the bed and landed on him. He gasped and clutched his stomach.

Ava appeared and punched him in the chest and face. He tried to roll and grab at her but couldn't reach with Zoey sitting on his stomach.

Everything turned into a big blur of hitting and dust flying. Somehow Dave managed to shove Zoey off him. He lunged for Ava again, but Zoey jumped on him from behind and managed to pull one arm behind his back.

He flipped around and knocked Zoey to the ground. She landed on something hard, and dust flew into her mouth and nose. It took a moment to recover, and by then Dave had Ava's hands pinned down.

Zoey grabbed a fistful of his hair and yanked his head back as far as she could. He let go of Ava, but she couldn't pull him off her.

Ava sat up, punching and scratching Dave. Zoey held her grip on his hair, keeping his head back as far as it would go. Her arms ached more with each moment that passed. She wouldn't be able to hold on much longer.

He swore at them, struggling against them both.

Zoey's mind raced. Ava didn't look like she had much more energy than Zoey did. The likelihood of them knocking him out and being able to get away were waning by the moment.

She had to do something different. But what? She looked around, not getting any ideas. There were no more weapon options in this room than out there.

The ropes. They could tie him up, get away, and send the cops to find him, wrapped up like a present.

Zoey rose and stepped away.

Ava's eyes widened.

Zoey brought a finger to her lips, then mouthed, "Trust me."

Dave rolled closer to Ava and pinned her arms. "I shouldn't have given you so much freedom!"

She spit in his face.

Zoey spun around and bolted for the chair. The ropes all lay on the floor. She scrambled for them and raced back to the room, where Dave now had Ava cornered next to the bed.

Zoey held up the ropes, but Ava couldn't see around him. She ran toward him and dropped the ties on the ground just before pulling Dave away from Ava. Her muscles and joints burned, but she ignored them. Just until they had *him* restrained.

He spun around and bit her in the shoulder.

She gasped as the sharp pain radiated out from the area.

Dave hit her in the jaw, then the temple.

Zoey stumbled back, hardly able to think. Her body was starting to feel like mush. Lifting her arm would be impossible.

He was going to win. Then what? What would he do with them after this? Kill them? Torture them?

She couldn't let that happen. Ava needed to get back home to her parents, and Zoey needed to return to her family, too. No. Giving up wasn't an option. No matter how impossible it seemed.

If nothing else, everyone would know how much she'd fought for them and for Ava.

With one last burst of energy, Zoey threw herself at him, her fists flying. He grabbed one of her wrists—it stung something fierce because of the rope burns—but she fought him. She put everything into it, and they both crashed to the ground.

Dave landed on top of her and wrapped his hands around her neck. "I should've done this back at the school!" His grip tightened.

Zoey struggled to breathe. She wrapped her fingers around his wrists and pulled, but it did no good. She still couldn't get any air.

"Hey Dave!"

He turned toward Ava, who held a broken baseball bat. She swung it at his head but missed. He let go of Zoey's neck and stumbled backwards.

SEARCH

Alex bit back a yawn and rubbed his bleary eyes. He'd been staring at his laptop for what felt like days. It had probably only been two or three hours, but he hadn't taken his attention from it even once in that time.

He was determined to find something on Dave. Anything. He'd gone through his various social media profiles, at least what was public. There wasn't much to gather.

The prick posted mostly bragging posts about his travels. He'd been to every major continent and loved posting selfies. Especially at beaches with bikini-clad women in the background or right there with him.

With two hours of searching, Alex hadn't been able to find a single post about being anywhere near Washington state. It was kind of strange, actually. He'd posted pictures practically everywhere else.

But not the area he chose to attack a school? It was almost too convenient.

Alex scrolled down more. He had to be close to a post that would give a useful clue. Or there weren't any, and he was wasting his time. The screen turned blurry, or rather, his vision did.

He got up and stretched. As much as he didn't want to take a break, he needed to. After walking around and eating a quick snack, he went back to the computer and took a deep breath.

Maybe Nick had learned something. He pulled out his phone and wandered over to the window, listening to it ring. Alex stared outside, focusing on evergreens in the distance.

Nick's voicemail came on, instructing him to leave a message.

"Hey, it's me. Just checking in. Call me." Alex ended the call and stared at the screen.

There had to be something more he could do. He'd already written a quick blog post about the incident, pleading with his readers to get the word out. With Dave being a flight attendant, he might have had an easier time getting out of state than most. The three of them could be anywhere. Anywhere.

Alex's stomach lurched. And Dave had shown that he had no problem killing adults. But why take Zoey? And leave her bloody shirt behind? Did he think she would take care of Ava? Or did he have much darker plans?

Anger burned in his gut, knowing the answer. Dave hadn't taken Zoey to be a babysitter. She was gorgeous—always had been—and any man would be lucky to catch her eye. Alex had managed to do that twice, even after screwing everything up so bad for so long.

Alex shook just thinking about what Dave could do to her while wielding a gun. Alex would rip off his head personally if he so much as laid a finger on her for any reason.

He stared at the trees in the distance for a few more minutes to make up for looking at the screen so long. Then when he couldn't wait a moment longer, he went back to the laptop.

This time, instead of continuing to scroll through Dave's feed, Alex opened a new tab and found Dave's pervy son Mason's profile. The kid also liked posting about places he'd visited. Not nearly as many as his dad, but plenty more than the average kid his age. Certainly far more than Alex had ever traveled.

He appeared to have no mom. Either that, or she had no online presence for him to connect to. That was more likely. The kid also didn't seem to have a girlfriend. Probably why he went after Ava. He couldn't get anyone to go near him without force.

Alex continued scrolling, quickly losing interest. Aside from his travel pictures, it was mostly all just normal, boring teenage boastings. The kind of things Alex himself had posted but had long since outgrown.

After ten more minutes, his eyes grew heavy. He was about ready to close the tab when something caught his attention. It was a picture of father and son in the woods together, both decked out in full camouflage hunting gear.

But that wasn't all. The woods, with the evergreens and mountains in the background, looked like they could be local.

The police could use that picture to figure out where those two were. There might be a cabin nearby, or maybe they have pictures of a camper—or anyplace Dave may have taken Zoey and Ava.

Alex could hardly breathe as he scrolled to find more pictures. There weren't any—at least not publicly. What if he sent a request? Did most kids still accept anyone as friends just to boost their numbers and look popular?

There was only one way to find out. He opened another tab and requested to connect with him. After there was no immediate acceptance, he went back to scrolling through the kid's feed. More boring brag-fests.

What about more pictures of hunting in the northwest? Alex's scrolling finger was starting to ache, but now that he'd actually found something useful, he was more determined than ever.

After another twenty minutes of scrolling—and nearly getting dizzy—Alex gave up. He walked around and drank an energy drink, stopping at his window to study the horizon. The mountains weren't within sight, so he had no way of knowing if that was the direction they'd been.

He checked again, but the request hadn't been accepted. What next? More scrolling? His head and finger hurt just thinking about it.

Instead, he tried calling Nick again. Then he texted him.

I think I found something big. Call me.

Alex went back to his laptop and downloaded the picture just to be safe. He wasn't going to risk one of them realizing their mistake and deleting it.

A little voice in his head told him to call the department, but after wasting their time with Flynn's sketch, Alex wanted to make certain he had something before going back to them with anything. He couldn't give them any reason to ignore what he had.

Back to scrolling it was.

EPIPHANY

Nick popped a couple ibuprofen in his mouth and downed them with hot black coffee. He glanced around the quaint coffee shop.

Everything was so normal. People were coming and going. Kids shrieked. Some friends laughed at something on a phone's screen. A guy complained about his boss.

The normalcy of everything was like a kick in the gut. There was nothing normal about life right now. Not with his daughter missing. Not with him unable to do anything about it.

He was living a nightmare while everyone around him was going about business as usual. It felt like an assault to what Ava was going through. Not only that, but an assault on the pain so many others were dealing with in the aftermath of the shooting. Kids missing their principal, nurse, secretary, and other loved adults. Teachers missing their coworkers. Families missing loved ones they'd never see again. They were the ones to really pity. Nick at least stood a fighting chance at finding his little girl— though she'd likely glare at him and have some choice words for him thinking of her as his little girl.

Nick smiled a little, thinking of her feistiness. Hopefully Ava was using her quick wit and internal strength to get herself away from Dave. If anyone could do it, it was her.

His phone buzzed in his pocket. Again. It had been going off constantly. So many people wanted to express their condolences, but as much as he really did appreciate it, he didn't want to talk to anyone about it. He only wanted to speak with anyone who had information that could help them find Ava. And so far, nobody knew anything helpful.

Nick pulled out the phone and glanced at the list of missed calls. The only person he remotely wanted to talk to was Alex, but given that Zoey was missing, he probably only wanted to know if Nick had learned anything, which he hadn't.

He then scrolled through the list of texts. Mostly everyone expressing their pity. No surprise there. He was just about to turn off the phone's screen when Alex's last message caught his attention.

He'd found something?

Nick's mind raced. He breathlessly called his friend back.

"Finally!" Alex answered.

"What did you find?" He held his breath as Alex explained the picture. "Text it to me, then let Garcia know."

"It would sound better coming from you."

"I'm off the case. You need to do this. Besides, you're the one who found it."

Alex groaned. "They think I'm an idiot."

"They're not going to ignore what could be solid evidence. If anyone does think poorly of you, this could change their minds."

"You think so?"

"I'm sure of it. Don't forget to send it to me. I want to see it."

"I thought you were off the case."

Nick took a deep breath. "Don't start with me."

"Hey, I wasn't trying to—never mind. I'll send you the picture. Want me to let you know what they say?"

"Yeah, let me know." Nick ended the call, his mind racing

worse than before. The headache medicine hadn't yet kicked in, turning the dull pain into a thundering roar.

A few seconds later, he got the picture. It was definitely Mason, and Nick would put money on the forest being local—or at the very least in the Pacific Northwest, maybe Oregon or Idaho. Possibly Alaska.

Corrine might know something. She was staying pretty tight-lipped about Dave, but maybe a look of shock on her face would confirm Nick's suspicions that she knew more than she was letting on.

He finished the drink, dropped the empty cup in the garbage, and headed back for his Mustang.

Parker and Hanna were out in the front yard, kicking a soccer ball back and forth. Neither appeared into it.

"Daddy!" Hanna ran over and threw her arms around him as soon as he stepped onto the sidewalk. "Are you picking us up today?"

Nick picked her up and kissed the top of her head. "I wish, sweetheart." He carried her over to Parker and gave him a hug. Parker didn't resist, even out in his yard where people could see. "I have to talk to your mom. Why don't you two go over to Shelly's?"

The young mom next door often babysat the kids. Normally, Parker would grumble about being watched, but they both headed over to her house without fussing.

While Nick appreciated the cooperativeness, he missed Parker's arguing. He was clearly beaten down by everything—not just his sister's disappearance but the shooting, and the fact that his mom's ex was the perpetrator. All three kids would need counseling.

Nick frowned, then watched as the neighbor welcomed them with hugs and brought them inside. He groaned as he ambled to the front door and knocked.

Corrine opened the door and her expression soured. "Oh, it's you again."

"Don't pretend to be excited for my benefit."

She glared at him. "What do you want, Nick?"

"I have just one more question."

"Can't get enough of me, can you?" She moved aside, then closed the door behind them.

Nick took his spot at the couch, but this time didn't kick his feet up.

"What do you want to know?" Corrine didn't sit.

"I need to show you something first." He patted the cushion next to him.

She eyed him with suspicion. "What?"

"Come and see."

"I don't have time for games. My daughter is missing!" She walked over to the window. "Where'd those kids go?"

"I sent them over to Shelly's so we could talk."

Corrine shot him an icy stare, then reluctantly sat next to him. "Hurry up."

Nick pulled out his phone and thought about what to say, but then figured he'd let the photo speak for itself. Without a word, he clicked it so that it took up the whole screen, then he handed it over.

Her eyes widened and her face paled. She covered her mouth with her free hand.

That confirmed it. She knew more than she was letting on.

"What?" Nick demanded.

Corrine looked up at him, her eyes shining with unshed tears.

He hadn't expected that. "What?"

She cleared her throat. "I just... I don't know what to say."

"How about start with why you're having such a strong reaction to the picture?" Nick leaned closer to her. He could smell her floral perfume. It was the same one she'd always worn.

"I... it's unnerving to see Dave after what he's done. He just looks so normal."

Nick studied the man. His jaw was jutted and his expression was gruff. "Normal?"

"Yeah." Corrine studied at the photo of the two and swallowed.

"He looks pretty serious. I thought you said he was a jokester."

Corrine narrowed her eyes. "I never said that. He has a sense of humor, that's what I said."

Nick shrugged. "So, which is the normal Dave? Funny or intimidating?"

"Both." She turned her attention back to the image. A different expression came over her face. Nick couldn't place it. Longing? Regret?

"Do you miss him?"

Corrine looked up at him. "What?"

"Dave. Do you miss him?"

"No. I was happy to leave him behind. He's kind of... suffocating."

Nick scratched his chin. "You didn't like someone giving you a lot of attention? I'd think you would since all I ever heard from you was that I never gave you enough."

"Did you come over here to pick on me while I'm already down?"

Guilt stung him, despite everything she'd done to hurt him. "No, sorry."

"You are?" She sounded so shocked.

Did she really see him as so cruel that he wouldn't be sorry for hurting her?

They stared at each other for a few moments until she glanced down at the picture and sighed. Nick followed her gaze to see if she was staring at the background or Dave. Her attention was fixated on his kid.

Nick studied him. Then something struck him. Sent a wave of disgust straight to his core. Mason's eyes were the same shape as Corrine's. He had her cheekbones. They even had the same mouth shape.

She looked up at him, and her eyes widened. "What?"

"He's your kid, isn't he? That's why you've been defending him."

TRUTH

ick's entire body shook as he stared at his ex-wife. Their entire relationship had been a lie. All those years. Everything he'd given her, including himself.

Now it made sense why it was never enough.

He jumped up from the couch and clenched his fists, staring down at her. "Answer me!"

She flinched, then nodded. "Yes."

Nick's stomach lurched, threatening to release the coffee and ibuprofen. "Mason's your kid?"

Corrine nodded, now looking away.

His mind spun, trying to make sense of it. How had she hidden a pregnancy from him? The kid had to have been conceived when they were together. At his age, that was the only thing that made sense.

"How did you keep this from me?"

"Nick, sit."

"No!"

She took a deep breath. "You have to calm down if you want me to tell you anything."

"Calm down?" he shouted. "You expect me to calm down?"

"I'm not going to tell you anything while you're intimidating me."

"You think this is intimidation? Screw it, I'll just take you to the station and you can explain why you kept information from them in such a big case! How about that? Obstruction of justice. Protecting a murderer."

"You'd do that to me?"

"Why not? Your lies could have cost us finding Ava! Speaking of lies, does your firstborn know he sexually assaulted his sister?"

"Stop saying that!"

"At least now I know why you've been defending that little pervert. Now it all makes sense."

Corrine glared at him.

"Tell me why you hid this from me," Nick demanded.

"After you sit."

"You don't get to call the shots."

She took a deep breath. "I first met Dave at a club when I was visiting Chelsea in New York."

"Your college roommate?"

Corrine nodded. "I was drunk, and you and I had just had a big fight. I didn't mean to sleep with him, but I did. And I hated myself for it the next morning. I called you as soon as I calmed down, and we made up."

"What was the fight?"

"I don't know. It seemed like the end of the world at the time, but now I can't even remember."

Nick bit his tongue. If he said what he felt like, he would regret it later. "Go on."

She squirmed in her seat. "Won't you sit?"

"No." He started pacing. "What happened next?"

Corrine picked at a nail. "I forgot about Dave and focused on you. On us. Then one day I realized I hadn't had a period in a couple of months. I took the test, but already knew the results before I got them."

"And you didn't think to tell me?"

She stared at him, her face pale. "I was terrified of losing you. I thought about telling you it was yours, but there was no way it would work with the timeframe. Between my travels and your obsession with the academy, we'd gone too long. You'd know right away."

Nick drew in a deep breath. "That year when you went to take care of your sick grandma."

Her eyes shone. "It was an outright lie. Once I started showing, I made that up and stayed with Chelsea. I was going to stay with her until I could adopt the baby out. Then I ran into Dave at the movies. He put two and two together, then said he wanted to raise the baby with me. I refused, wanting to get back to you. He convinced me to let him keep the baby—promised he'd never ask for money or give up my identity unless I wanted to be involved. Since he was the dad, I figured that was for the best. At least the baby would know one parent."

Nick fell onto the couch, unable to stand any longer as he took in the story. "You gave up your kid?"

She wiped her eyes. "So I could be with you. I never wanted to be apart from you. Our daily video chats weren't enough for the short time I was away. I knew I couldn't live without you. Once the baby was born, I didn't even hold him. I didn't want to become attached. So, Dave took him, then as soon as I could work out, I got myself back into shape and came back here."

He stared at her. "If you were so desperate to be with me, then why did you divorce me? I pleaded. You know I did, since you love to throw that fact in my face."

"I never got to see you! Your real wife is the force, and you know it. Spending time with our kids made me realize how much I was missing out on my other son's life. Once I figured out that I couldn't have you, not really, then I knew I needed to have all my kids together. As much as I wanted to believe you would change, I knew you wouldn't. I had to leave and get to know my child."

Nick closed his eyes and leaned his head against the couch. Everything made sense. Any questions he had, now they were answered.

There were so many things he wanted to ask her, but he had no energy. Questions like was it worth it? Did the kid know Ava's his sister? Was that why Corrine was convinced he'd never touch Ava again?

Then another question struck him—were Nick's kids his?

He sat upright and turned to her. "Are our kids mine?"

Corrine's eyes widened. "Yes! Of course. How could you ask that?"

Nick glared at her.

"You're all I ever wanted, Nick! I gave up my baby to be with you! Yes, our kids are yours. Test their paternity. You'll see."

He grabbed his phone from her and stared at the picture of Dave, trying to find any similarities between him and the kids. There were none with Ava and Hanna. But Parker...

Parker had been born not long after he and Corrine had gone through the roughest patch of their marriage. They'd even separated for a short while.

Nick glared at her. "You sure about that?"

"Yes!"

"Was Parker conceived during our separation?"

Her mouth dropped.

"Was he?"

"Right before. I swear."

"Forgive me if I don't believe you. Where did you go when we were separated? Back to Dave?"

Corrine shook her head.

"Or did he come here? Is that it? You two hooked up right under my nose?"

"No!"

"Maybe I will take you up on that paternity test."

She looked down at her lap. "You'll find that I'm telling the truth."

"We'll see, won't we?"

Corrine didn't reply.

"Tell me one thing."

"What?"

"Do you know anything about where he has Ava?"

"If I knew anything, I'd tell you. I'd have told the cops who were here earlier. The only thing I want is to have her back in my arms!"

That last part was the one thing he could believe. He hoped he was right to trust her. "If you think of anything else, tell someone. Don't protect him."

"I wouldn't. Not after this."

"Good." Nick marched to the door but turned back to her before twisting the knob. "One more question."

"What is it?" She'd never looked more defeated than that moment.

"Why didn't you bring your son with you back here?"

"Would you have let our girls stay with me if I had?"

They both knew the answer to that. "Were you hoping we still stand a chance?"

She looked away. "Just go, Nick."

"Where is Mason now?"

"I don't want to talk about this right now."

He slammed the door and marched over to her. "I'm not trying to annoy you. He's a danger to our daughter. I have a right to know if he's in the area."

She shook her head. "Mason's staying with his grandma. He had to switch schools after the show you made when you flew out there."

Nick lowered himself to her level and stared her down. "Is he going to be a problem for Ava?"

"Ava has bigger problems right now, or have you forgotten?"

He resisted the urge to slap her across the face. "I'm talking about when she gets back. Is Mason going to be anywhere near our daughter?"

"No, and he's horrified about feeling up his sister. We really should have told him sooner."

"You think?" Nick glowered at her before heading back to the door. Once his hand was on the knob, he turned around. "Does Mason know anything about this whole mess?"

"He's a teenager. The kid spends more time online than not."

Nick clenched his jaw. "I mean about his father."

Corrine shook her head. "He thinks he's over here working things out with me."

Fury ran through him. He needed to get out of the house before he said or did something he would surely regret.

LEAD

Genevieve glanced back at her phone. Still nothing from Nick. Not that she should expect anything, given everything he was dealing with. She was being ridiculous thinking that returning her calls and texts would even remotely be a priority.

She turned back to the computer screen and continued going over the evidence file she'd been assigned for another case. With so many others helping, their department was able to focus on the local stuff.

It was almost time to go home once she filed the related paperwork. Then the phone on her desk rang.

Genevieve groaned. If she answered it, it would likely mean more work. If she didn't, she could go home and collapse. After she picked up Tinsley at the neighbor's apartment.

She yawned, just thinking about having to do anything other than sleeping. But she wasn't the type of person to avoid the calls. No, she did what she was supposed to, because it was the right thing.

She answered, expecting one of the detectives dumping some of their work onto her. What she wasn't expecting was the frantic voice on the other end of the line. She couldn't even understand the man.

"Can you slow down, sir? I'm not sure what you're saying."

The guy on the other end took a deep breath. "I'm jogging in the woods down near the valley. You know the area?"

"By the winery?"

"Yeah, back that way. I saw two women. Well, actually one woman and one young girl. I think they're those missing people from the middle school! They look just like them!"

Genevieve's heart jumped into her throat. Why was he calling the local police number, rather than the hotline or nine-one-one? But this was her chance. What if she could be the one to find Nick's daughter?

She shoved aside her selfish thoughts. "What did they look like? What were they wearing?"

He went on to describe long dark hair for both, a tank top for one, and a rock band t-shirt for the other. "I'm pretty sure neither had any shoes."

Genevieve had to take a couple deep breaths to calm herself. It sounded like a solid lead. "Did you talk to them?"

"No, they ran the other way when they saw me."

They must've been spooked. It made sense. "Can you see them now, sir?"

"No. They took off, like I said."

"Okay. Stay where you are. Officers are heading over there." She got his name and number, then ran over to Detective Anderson and explained everything.

His eyes widened, and he called out orders.

Genevieve cleared her throat. "I'd like to go, too."

Anderson threw her a sideways glance.

"I can do this. Why do you think the captain goes with me so often?"

He opened his mouth, then shut it. "Okay. Go with Mackey. She knows that area well. Grant and I will be behind you."

Genevieve nodded. "Thank you, Detective."

A few minutes later, she and Mackey were on the road, lights flashing. Her heart always raced in times like this. She hoped the thrill never dulled.

Even with everyone moving out of their way, it seemed to take forever to get to the valley. Could those two people in the woods actually be Ava and Zoey? Had they gotten away from the gunman, or had he let them go to send a message?

"You talked to the caller?" Mackey asked.

"Yes." She explained what the two women were wearing.

"Okay. There are a lot of paths in that part of the forest. Is Anderson sending the canines?"

"He didn't say."

"Call him and tell him the dogs need to at least be ready to go. This could turn into a full-scale search with so much ground to cover."

"Okay." She spoke with Anderson, who was already on it. "Everything is set."

"Good." Mackey pulled onto a dirt road that made a roller-coaster at the county fair feel like a smooth ride.

After some sharp turns, they came to an open field. The winery was down below in the distance. Mackey pulled next to an old green pickup.

A man waved to them from the edge of the trees.

"Must be our guy." Mackey called in their arrival and a description of the man.

They hurried out to meet the guy in full workout gear. He took a deep breath and explained the path the women had taken.

"I know exactly where that is." Mackey nodded. "Stay here. Others are right behind us."

Genevieve and Mackey ran into the dark woods. The other officer darted around the maze-like paths like a pro. Before long, they came to a fork.

Mackey stopped and took a deep breath. "This is where it's

going to get tricky. If they went to the left, they're going to come to the cliff leading down to the winery. It's not impossible to get down, but it is dangerous. Especially without gear. The other way leads deep into the woods. Could be where they came from, and if that's the case, I doubt they'd go there."

"Should we split up?"

"Yeah, we'd better. Head toward the cliff, and if you find any clues, I'll join you. I'm going to go this way and see if I can find anything indicating that's the way they came. Whether we do or don't find clues, we'll meet back here."

"Sounds good."

Mackey darted down the path to the right. Genevieve watched as she disappeared. Her heart thundered. She hated the woods. People went there to do terrible things.

She shoved aside the memories that not even years of therapy could help her forget and started down the path. Her skin crawled as though someone was watching her.

It was ridiculous. Nobody was watching her. The people who'd hurt her were locked behind bars, and she had them to thank for her career choice.

She squeezed her gun, ready to shoot at a moment's notice.

Twigs crunched underfoot and bushes rustled as she squeezed through the narrow path. It was impossible to stay quiet. If the women were out this way, they'd hear her coming a mile away. Anyone else would hear her, too.

Genevieve stopped and closed her eyes. Nobody else was out there. There were no monsters in the shape of a human waiting for her. She opened her eyes and continued down the path.

A few minutes later, light shone from the trail. She raced toward it, finding herself at the top of a steep cliff. Nobody was climbing down. As far as Genevieve could tell, nobody was anywhere nearby.

She pressed her back against a tree and glanced around, paying special attention to the shadows. Looking for anything out of place.

Nothing.

She drew a deep breath. It was time to head back. Maybe Mackey had found something.

Snap!

Her throat closed up. She had no idea where the breaking branch had come from. Given the trees and the cliff, sound carried differently.

It could be anywhere.

Why had she agreed to this? She hadn't thought she'd be alone in the woods. But she should've known better.

Snap!

She needed to pull herself together. As an officer of the law, protecting citizens was her duty. If Ava and Zoey were out there, most likely terrified, they needed Genevieve at the top of her game. Not scared of monsters that weren't there.

Holding her breath, she aimed the gun in front of her, ready to spin in any direction at a moment's notice.

Snap!

Genevieve turned to the left. The noise had definitely come from there. Her pulse drummed in her ears, making it impossible to listen.

She stepped away from the tree and crept toward the direction of the sound. Her skin crawled. The hairs on the back of her neck stood on end.

Why had she thought this was a good idea? She didn't need to be the hero. Nick would either like her or not like her regardless of who found his daughter.

Snap!

Her trigger finger twitched, but she stopped herself from shooting.

"Who's there?"

Silence.

Genevieve's skin felt afire. Her mouth was dry.

She narrowed her eyes and studied the darkened path. The shadow of the trees made it feel like the middle of the night. What little light came from the cliff only gave everything an eerie glow.

Rustle, rustle.

It was closer. And definitely to the left.

Once again holding her breath, Genevieve crept toward the noise.

More rustling noises sounded in the same direction.

She pressed through some bushes and ducked under low-hanging branches. One caught in her ponytail. She stopped and yanked it, but it wouldn't pull free.

Genevieve worked to untangle her tresses, but it was stuck. She'd have to deal with it later. She snapped the branch and pushed her way through the thick plants.

Rustle, rustle.

The noises were closer. This was the right direction.

She gripped her weapon tighter and pressed on as the rustling grew louder. They were hard to hear over her own nerves and moving aside the bushes and branches.

Genevieve came to a small clearing. It was barely big enough for a picnic blanket. And there were the two people matching the description given to him. All she could see was their long dark hair as they made out on the forest floor.

Relief flooded through her that nobody was after her, but then a new worry shot fear through her. What if the shooter was forcing Zoey and Ava to suck face while he hid, watching? Watching Genevieve, too?

She glanced around, not seeing anyone. Not that it offered her much comfort. He could be hiding anywhere.

"Stop! Police!"

The two women turned to her, eyes wide. Only it wasn't two women. The "girl" with the rock band shirt was actually a guy with long hair. He was a teenager, and the woman, a teacher. Genevieve recognized her.

"On your feet!"

"How'd you find us?" asked the kid. "We were careful!"

Genevieve shoved the gun closer. "On your feet!"

They scrambled to stand.

She cuffed the teacher and read her the Miranda rights before ordering them back to the path.

Then she radioed Mackey. "I've got them, but they aren't who we were looking for. I did catch a predator, though."

FLEE

Ava leaned against the dirt-caked wall and slid to the floor. "I'm still hungry."

Zoey nodded. "So am I, but at least we had something. It'll help us get back home."

Ava nodded, but she didn't speak her fears. She didn't dare. Without shoes and with so little food in their stomachs, how far could they really go? This little cabin felt like it was in the middle of nowhere.

Plus she was so tired on top of being hungry still. Everything ached, especially her ankles. Even with the handcuffs off, they still hurt something fierce. They'd dug into her skin, leaving it raw and bleeding. Some of her flesh was barely hanging on.

Zoey dug through the fridge again, then the cabinets. They'd shared a half-eaten sandwich and a container of bologna. It had been nowhere near enough.

She turned to Ava. "You ready?"

Ava rubbed her tender ankle, but let go as soon as pain shot out. "How long do you think it'll take to get back?"

Zoey frowned. "I have no idea. It took hours to get here in the car."

Ava clenched her fists. "Can I go in there and beat the crap out of him?"

"I think we'd be better off getting out of here."

"He'll go free!"

Zoey shook her head. "We'll tell the police about the cabin. He's tied up."

Ava shrugged. Their knots were nowhere near as tight as the ones Dave had used on them. He'd probably be able to get out before the cops could find the place.

"Come on."

Ava shook her head no. Now that Dave was taken care of, why did she feel like giving up? Had she exhausted herself fighting against him? "I'm so tired."

Zoey held out her hand to help her up. "I promise you, your parents will let you sleep all you want after this. We have to go now."

Deep down, Ava knew she was right. Reluctantly, she took Zoey's hand and rose to her feet.

"You can do this." Zoey locked gazes with her. "You can."

Ava thought about her friends and family. About Braylon, the quirky but adorable kid two doors down. She'd been afraid to tell him how she felt—even though nothing else scared her. If nothing else, she needed to get back and find out if he liked her back.

She turned her attention back to Zoey. "Let's do this."

"I saw a back door from that chair. We'll try that."

Ava nodded. Her heart pounded like a jackhammer. They crept over to it. A keg was pressed up against the door.

Dave hardly seemed like the kind of guy to have a kegger, but whatever. Between the two of them, they were able to move the heavy thing out of the way. The liquid inside sloshed around but didn't make enough noise that Dave would hear it from the bedroom.

Zoey reached for the knob.

Ava held her breath, half-expecting the cabin to blow up when she touched it.

It didn't.

She twisted, but it didn't move. Zoey twisted the lock and tried again.

The knob turned.

Ava nearly peed her pants. She breathed a sigh of relief.

Zoey twisted the knob further and pulled.

The door opened. They were just feet from freedom.

Ava's knees wobbled.

Zoey stepped outside, then waved Ava out.

She glanced back at the bedroom, expecting Dave to be standing there.

He wasn't.

She bolted outside, running past Zoey. Her ankles throbbed, but not enough to slow her. Rocks and branches dug into her soles. Nothing had ever felt better.

They were free!

Zoey caught up. They ran for a few minutes before Ava's bladder felt like it would explode.

"I need to stop."

"Already?"

"I have to pee!"

"Now that you mention it, so do I. Let's hurry." She ducked behind a cluster of trees.

Ava stepped behind a thick shrub, dropped her pants, and squatted. Luckily, she'd worn leggings. Easy to come off.

Sweet relief. She'd never had to hold it so long. Ava closed her eyes.

Snap!

Her eyes flew open. "Z-Zoey?"

"No," came the deep voice behind her.

Terror ripped through her and the stream of pee stopped.

"Don't quit on my account. Surely, you just came out here to relieve yourself. You wouldn't escape would you?"

"I... I..." Ava's mind raced to find a way to flee.

"Well, finish what you were doing. May as well. You're going to be inside for a long time, Ava."

That was where he was wrong. She would die fighting before she'd set foot back in that cabin.

"I'm waiting."

She needed to buy time. "I can't go with you watching."

"I'm not looking. I swear."

As much as she hated it, she would have to pee in front of him. It was the only way she could come up with an escape plan.

"Are you done yet?" Dave asked.

"Just turn around."

He laughed. "You must think I'm pretty stupid."

"Fine." She closed her eyes and pretended she was alone in a bathroom. The stream flowed again.

How was she supposed to get away with him so close and her pants around her knees?

The only thing that made any sense would be to jump up mid-pee and run, pulling her pants up as she went. She had to try.

She was almost done, so there wasn't any time to waver.

Ava jumped up. Urine streamed down her leg and soaked into her pants. She ran, reaching for the waistband and pulled it up. Unfortunately, it also slowed her.

She stumbled as she yanked it on, and nearly crashed into a tree. But she managed to push off it and regain her balance. Her ankles continued to throb, but at least nothing was broken.

Fingers brushed against her arm.

Ava screamed. Then she ran faster.

The fingers grabbed her arm, this time squeezing tightly and yanking her back. Dave pulled on her hair, forcing Ava's head back.

"You're going to regret that." He was so close, she could feel his hot breath on her skin.

"Run, Zoey!"

He covered Ava's mouth. "Yeah, run! I have my gun! I'll shoot Ava if you come near us! If I see you again, I'll shoot you!"

Then he dragged her back toward the cabin.

She kicked and screamed, not that it did any good against him.

GUILT

Z oey fought the urge to run after Dave and Ava. If she tried to take him down, she would fail. He would shoot one of them. He'd already proven he had no problem killing people.

She couldn't risk Ava's life. What she needed to do was to get away and tell the police about this place. *They* could take him down.

But the question was, why did he want her to run? Was it to make her think twice, then go back? Or did he have another plan for Zoey? Like hunting her down as soon as he had Ava restrained again? Or did he think she would die before ever making it out of the woods because they were so deep?

Her head hurt. She had to think, though. There was no other option.

Dave had threatened to kill Ava if she came after them. She had to believe him. If he did kill the girl, it would be her fault. Then she'd never be able to look Alex's best friend in the eyes again.

No. There had to be a road nearby. She would find it and flag someone down. Tell them to call the cops.

Hopefully it wouldn't be too late. She couldn't risk Ava's life by going after her.

She listened but couldn't hear them anymore. Guilt stung for leaving without her, but she *would* find a way out of the woods.

Zoey shivered. It was time to move, she couldn't let anything slow her down—not being cold, hungry, or lost. None of that was an option.

She cupped her ears, but still didn't hear anything.

Now it was time to move, but which direction? It was nothing more than a guess.

She closed her eyes and whispered a quick prayer, hoping that might work.

A slight breeze tickled her skin and gave her goose bumps.

Her heart sped up. Was that a sign? Was she supposed to follow the direction of the breeze?

Zoey glanced to her left. There was a narrow path she hadn't noticed before.

She bolted for it.

"I'll get you help, Ava."

She ran as fast as she could without shoes. Everything dug into her feet—rocks, branches, and other sharp things she couldn't identify.

Dave probably thought she would never make it out of the woods alive. Not like she was. But that was where he was wrong. He'd just underestimated Zoey Carter, and he would spend the rest of his life in jail because of it. She would see to that.

NOWHERE

Alex struggled to keep his eyes open. It had been hours since he'd sent the photo of Dave and his kid to Nick and Detective Garcia, hearing nothing back from anyone.

He'd also managed to find absolutely nothing more with his online searching. It would take either getting a lot more creative or getting one of them to accept him as a friend online, and being that he was connected to Nick, it was unlikely.

His mouth was dry, so he grabbed an energy drink and turned on the news. Maybe there was some big break in the case that nobody had told him about. His picture could have led the police to the cabin.

Yeah, it was probably too soon for that, but Alex couldn't look at his laptop for another moment. He sipped his drink and flipped through the channels until he came to the first news report.

They were covering the shooting at the scene. Of course they were zooming in on the part of the building that had been blown up. Nobody had been hurt in the blast, but that looked most dramatic.

A sketch of Dave, the one that looked the most like him, and the reporter switched the topic to him. His name and other details about him scrolled on the ticker at the bottom, and they were asking anyone with details to call the hotline or their local police station.

After that, they showed several actual pictures of him—all ones that Alex had already seen. Ones easily accessible from Dave's online presence. Nothing about the cabin or his kid.

The police had to keep some stuff secret from the public to help weed out real and fake tips, and that was probably what they'd picked.

Alex flipped to the other news stations, finding pretty much the same thing on all channels. He stopped cold when he saw an image of Flynn in a crowd of people near the school as police continued to process the scene.

Alex jumped up and yelled at the screen to go back. He pulled out his phone, ready to snap a picture of the image. But they didn't return to the crowd. That would be the proof he needed that Flynn was actually a free man. Maybe he and Nick could find the footage online.

He was about to turn the TV off when the last news reporter said something that made Alex's stomach twist.

"The suspect is tied to the local police captain. I did some digging and found that Dave Cooper was dating Captain Nicholas Fleshman's ex-wife. He has no prior criminal history, but his son on the other hand—"

Alex turned off the TV and took a deep breath. It was probably only a matter of time until all of that came out, and Alex didn't want to be the one to tell Nick. But they were friends. He couldn't let Nick find out everything was out there from someone else, much less the cold news itself.

He went back to his spot at the window and stared out at the night sky. "Fight, Zoey. Keep fighting."

It took a minute to build the nerve to call Nick and tell him the connection had been made. The news was probably already spreading, and quickly.

Not surprisingly, Alex got Nick's voicemail. He hung up and texted him.

One of the news stations figured out your connection to Dave. Call me.

After hitting send, Alex regretted being so direct. He hadn't meant to drop the bomb on his friend through a text. Too late now.

What?

Call me.

Alex's phone rang.

"Hey, sorry to tell you over text."

"No, I get it. I wouldn't have responded otherwise. Which station? How do they know?"

"I think it was one of the national ones. Sorry, I wasn't paying attention. It pissed me off, so I just had to walk away."

"That wasn't supposed to be released to the press. Someone had to leak the information."

"The reporter said she figured it out. Probably sniffing out his online presence."

"Wouldn't be too hard, now that you mention it. I think Parker is connected to both of us. Ava cut all ties." Nick's tone sounded off.

Alex couldn't figure out what exactly it was. Obviously, he was crazy worried for Ava, but there was something else. "Are you okay?"

Nick drew in a deep breath, then released it slowly. He didn't say anything.

Something was definitely up—something he wasn't telling Alex.

"Hey, if you want to talk—"

"I don't."

Laughter sounded in the background.

"Where are you?"

"Nowhere."

"How can you be nowhere?"

Nick sighed. "I'm actually at the Nowhere Bar and Grill. Trying to think. It's not working."

"Mind if I join you?"

"Why not? Misery loves company, right?"

"Sure does. See you in a few."

On his way over, Alex realized Nick was at the bar and grill. Given Alex's past struggles, he hoped his friend was at the restaurant side of the establishment. If not...

He shook his head. They could always move if Nick was there. No big deal.

The thought of alcohol sent a rush of desire through him. It pushed on him like a lead weight.

With Zoey missing, he wasn't sure he could handle the temptation. But Nick knew about his struggles. He would help him say no. Or would he? With his own misery, Alex's struggle with the drink would be the furthest thing from his mind. Probably why he'd invited him to the bar in the first place.

That was also why Alex had immediately thought to decline.

Alex clenched the steering wheel. Maybe he should just turn around. He wasn't sure he could beat his demons this night. Not at a bar.

Just the thought of being surrounded by boisterous drinkers made his mouth water for a beer. Or some shots of something stronger.

That sounded so good. It would *feel* so good.

Only one. Well, maybe two. Just as long as he didn't get drunk.

Everybody would understand, given the circumstances. It wasn't like he was going to return to old habits. He just needed some relief. To blow off some steam.

No big deal.

Alex stopped at a traffic light and closed his eyes, imagining the way it would feel going down.

A text came in. Alex pulled himself away from the fantasy to check it. It was from Nick.

Hey, let's meet at the coffee shop next door. I could really use some caffeine.

Alex took a deep breath. Thank God for good friends.

There was no way he could only have one or two drinks. It would lead to so much more. Potentially ruining everything if he spiraled far enough out of control.

He texted Nick back. *Yeah. If that's what you want. Almost there.*

I do. See you in a few. I'll order you a mocha.

Thanks.

Hopefully Nick understood the gratitude Alex couldn't find words to express.

SURPRISE

Nick waved to Alex from the back of the dim coffee shop. He shoved the enormous peppermint mocha toward the empty seat. Guilt stung him for his momentary lapse of judgment. Inviting his recovering alcoholic friend to a bar.

He was such an idiot. At least he'd come to his senses before Alex came in. Normally Alex would've declined, and it worried Nick that he hadn't.

Neither of them said anything about Nick's stupidity as Alex sat. "How much do I owe you for this?"

"Nothing." Nick sipped his black coffee. "So, word's out about Dave's relationship with Corrine?"

"Unfortunately."

He took a deep breath. "I suppose it was only a matter of time."

"I guess." Alex guzzled the hot drink like it was his lifeline.

"At least I'm not only off the case but taking leave. Nobody can make any false claims."

"Well, your daughter's missing. Who could blame you?"

Nick nodded. "No way I could get any work done. I'm next to useless. Don't know how I managed with you gone."

Alex set the cup down. "It's different, I get it. Ava's your *kid*. There's nothing worse."

"But still, I was worried as hell when you were abducted."

"I know."

They sat in silence, sipping their caffeine, trying to avoid getting too touchy-feely. Words weren't necessary. They were friends, and they had each other's backs. It wasn't like they needed to talk about it.

After a few minutes, Alex tapped the table. "You sure you're okay? You sounded... I don't know, different on the phone."

Nick drew in a deep breath. He'd rather tell Alex he loved him like a brother than talk about how stupid he'd been to be with Corrine all those years, much less to mention the possibility of any of his kids being Dave's. He'd happily throw her under the bus about being Mason's mother if it didn't make Nick look like such a fool.

Alex spun his empty cup on the table. "You don't have to tell me, but I'm here. I know how hard it is to have a missing kid."

Nick nodded and dug his nail into a groove in the table. "I appreciate it."

He probably would tell Alex all about it, eventually. Now just wasn't the time. Or was it? What if word got out about Corrine's first child? It wasn't out of the realm of possibility.

What if Corrine's college friend put two and two together? She could sell the entire humiliating story to a news source—for a lot of money with a case this high profile. Then the whole world would know their dirty laundry. How naive and foolish the police captain really was.

He looked up at Alex, who gave him a sympathetic glance.

May as well tell him. At least he would have someone to talk to about the mess. Alex wouldn't judge.

Nick took a deep breath. "Corrine is Mason's mom."

Alex's eyes widened as he processed the news. "You mean Dave's kid?"

Nick nodded.

"Like you mean, she gave birth to him? Not like she adopted him?"

Nick nodded. "Corrine kept it from me all these years."

"Oh, man. While you were together?"

"Yeah. Pretty stupid of me, huh?"

"How's that possible? I get a guy being able to hide something like that, but a woman?"

Nick studied the groove in the table. "She went across the country to take care of her grandma, except that was a lie. Can you believe that when she came back I didn't even notice she'd been pregnant and had a baby?"

"I'm so sorry, Nick."

"You'd think I'd notice something like that, but she did a good job of getting back into shape. It also helped her that she never got stretch marks until Hanna."

"She gave up the baby?"

"Let him raise it because she was afraid of losing me. Can you believe she went to all that trouble to pull one over on me? And I fell for it. Hook, line, and sinker. Then, of course, when she got tired of me, she ran right back to Dave."

The discussion made Nick's head spin. They talked in circles about the whole disaster, and at least Alex didn't think Nick was an idiot.

After a while, one of the baristas came over and told them the cafe was closing.

Alex yawned and stretched. "I should probably get a few hours of shut-eye."

"Yeah, same here." Nick rose, feeling like his body was a lead weight. He and Alex said their goodbyes at the door and headed to their separate cars.

Nick sat in his car and stared at the dashboard. Putting the key in the ignition felt like a monumental task. His arms may as well have been tied down.

Out of the corner of his eye, he watched Alex pull out of the parking lot. Nick sighed. What did he have to go home to? An empty condo with no food, full of despair. It was like an open grave, waiting to swallow him whole.

What would he do if Dave hurt his baby girl? If that monster laid a hand on her?

If Nick had never been so stupid as to miss the fact that his fiancée had given birth to someone else's baby, none of them would be in this mess. No. If Corrine hadn't been a heartless cheater, then none of this would've happened. That kid wouldn't have been born, and she wouldn't have felt the need to run back to Dave.

Nick leaned his head against the steering wheel. He needed to stay strong, but he'd never felt weaker. He didn't think he could ever move from his spot again.

He wasn't sure how much time had passed when his phone rang. Probably Alex.

Nick reached for it, not moving his head from its place on the steering wheel. It was Corrine. He wanted to throw the phone through a window. That would take too much energy.

He accepted the call and put her on speaker. "What?"

"Nick, I found something. You need to see this."

"Did you discover another baby you forgot to tell me about? Is this one a serial killer?"

A beat of silence passed before she spoke. "Nick, I'm serious. I—"

"I'm serious, Corrine."

"Look, I already told you everything. But I was going through some pictures and found one that I must've accidentally brought back from Dave's."

"I don't want to see your kinky photos."

"Nick! That's not what I'm talking about. I found a picture of a cabin. Looks like it could be from around here. Maybe he took Ava there."

He sat up. "Why are you telling me? Call Anderson or Garcia. Anyone who's actually on the case!"

"Okay, but I want you to see it. I want to know what you think."

"I'll be there in a few minutes." He ended the call and started the car. It didn't make any sense that she wanted him to see it before showing the police, but if it could help bring Ava home, he'd go back to Corrine's place.

Her house was dark and quiet.

"Parker and Hanna are sleeping."

"That's good. How are they holding up?"

"It's rough. Parker isn't as easy to convince that everything's going to be okay, but Hanna's holding out hope."

At least someone was. "Where's the picture?"

"Right over here." She led him to the couch and picked up a shoe box. "I grabbed a bunch of pictures from his place, wanting some of my boy."

Nick's stomach twisted hearing her call Mason hers. Yes, it was true, but it hadn't really sunk in yet. He turned on a lamp and sat next to her. "Let me see the picture of the cabin."

She pulled it out, handed it to him, and then set the box on the other side of her. Tears welled in her eyes. "I just want this nightmare to be over."

Nick bit back a comment about it all being her fault and studied the picture. The dilapidated cabin seemed to be in the same woods as the picture Alex found—it was very similar. "Have you called the station about this?"

Corrine nodded and sniffled.

"Good." Nick handed her back the photo. "They can handle it. I don't know why I'm here."

"Nick, I need you. We're a family. You should be here with me and the kids."

He stared at her, unable to find words.

She scooted closer and pleaded with her eyes. "Move in here,

Nick. We won't have to bounce the kids back and forth. We can all be together all the time. I won't complain about your work hours, I promise."

"Don't you understand how divorce works?"

"It was a mistake. We can fix it." Corrine leaned closer and forced her mouth on his. She moved even closer, put her palms on his chest and pressed herself against him.

Nick was pinned against the corner of the couch. He put his hands on her shoulders to move her out of the way, but she took it wrong and climbed onto his lap, then deepened the kiss.

He shoved her off and jumped up. "What are you doing?"

"Baby, don't you miss that? How good we were together?"

"You're—"

Ding-dong!

He glared at her. "Don't ever do that again!"

"Nicky!"

He stormed to the door and flung it open. Garcia and Chang stood there, both with funny expressions.

Nick gestured to Corrine. "She has a photo you'll find interesting." Then he hurried past them without another word, heading straight for his Mustang.

TEMPTATION

Alex set down the black plastic basket. He shouldn't have come here. Yet he had.

He took a deep breath, his insides shaking as he stared at the beer. Rows and rows of it, all refrigerated to perfection.

"Excuse me." Two giggling blondes moved around him and took a couple bottles of fruit-flavored drinks. Whispering and laughing, they left.

Alex licked his lips and stared at his old favorite. The cheapest one there—the only thing he could afford back when he worked as a roofer in his smelly little apartment.

He could afford much better now, but his old friend called his name.

Really, would it be such a big deal if he had a drink? Was it wrong, or just a bad idea? It wasn't like alcohol was bad. Not in moderation. If he only bought one bottle—maybe two—then he couldn't have more. It would be just enough to dull the pain. He couldn't go through a whole box if he didn't *have* a box.

If the stuff was so bad, why did they sell it at the grocery store? It wasn't like it was illegal. He could take a couple bottles to the register and buy them, and nobody would bat an eye. It would be just another tired-looking guy bringing home some beer.

Except that he wasn't just some dude. He knew the path the drink would take him. He *knew*. But that didn't stop him from standing there, staring at all those bottles full of liquid sunshine. Or liquid hell.

But could just one bottle really be that bad? Just one?

Surely, he'd moved on far enough that he could handle it. Especially given everything in his life. His fiancée was being held by a madman. Maybe he'd already killed her.

A relaxing drink was practically required in a situation like this. People would think he was crazy *not* to.

As he stood there trying to figure out what to do, several others came by and grabbed various drinks. None were conflicted. Not one person gave it a second thought.

It wasn't bad stuff. All he needed was just enough to relax and get some sleep. That way he could be awake and alert tomorrow to dig up more dirt on Dave and Mason.

Alex reached for a bottle, then froze. If he did this, he'd have to start over with his number of days without alcohol. His mind was too fuzzy to think of what that number was, but it was in the hundreds. It was impressive and he'd worked hard to get there. And besides, he liked marking each day on his calendar.

Did he really want to throw that away for one drink?

He stared at the bottle. His mouth watered and his insides shook.

Did some arbitrary number really mean anything? Who really cared how many days he'd gone? Was he going to win an award? Have it proudly displayed on his gravestone?

It wasn't like there was some ticker on his forehead. Not that many people even knew about his past struggles.

He glanced at his shaking hand, frozen halfway to the beer bottle. *Past* struggles. That was laughable.

Except he wasn't laughing.

Beads of sweat broke out on his forehead.

This was getting ridiculous. It was just one drink. One.

He took a deep breath. Closed his eyes and pictured Ariana, safe but sick in her bed. He pictured his brand new nephew. The tiny baby he'd almost had to deliver.

Two children who he'd seen born. One who looked up to him and loved him. The other who hopefully would feel the same way.

He couldn't let them down.

Then there was Zoey. Scared somewhere. Probably hurt. Maybe worse. She was so proud of him for his long streak of no alcohol. So proud he could see it in her eyes.

He didn't want to let her down, either.

Alex opened his eyes. He stared down the bottles. "You aren't going to win today."

He picked up the shopping basket and headed for the bread aisle, where he'd originally been heading.

CRUSHED

G enevieve forced smiles as she made her way to her desk, a double-shot espresso in hand. She'd slept fitfully and had to face another day of work.

Not only was she worried about Nick—she'd stopped calling and texting—but now she was having flashbacks to her experience in the woods. And for what? She hadn't helped find Ava and Zoey. Yeah, she'd stopped a predatorial teacher, but it hardly felt like a win.

She sat and opened up her emails, hoping the distraction would help pull her out of the funk.

There was a slight buzz of excitement in the air. Hopefully, that meant there had been a break in the case that she hadn't heard about yet. Something the news hadn't gotten ahold of.

Genevieve gulped her coffee, hoping it would help. So far, nothing.

Chang came over and leaned against her desk, hovering over her. "Did you hear?"

She kept her gaze on the computer screen. "About what?"

He laughed. "Oh, I don't know. Some school shooting. Sound familiar?"

She glared at him. "Either tell me or leave me alone."

"Who pissed in your cereal this morning?"

It took all her self-control not to throw the rest of her espresso in his face.

The corners of his mouth twitched, then he leaned closer, still over her. "Well, the captain's ex is being really helpful in this case. We have a possible location for the cabin."

Genevieve's eyes lit up. "We do?"

He nodded and pressed his palm on her desk, inching closer to her. "Yeah, the feds have been on it all night. Just got the location a few minutes ago. But that's not the biggest news."

"There's more? Are the hostages okay?"

"We don't know yet, but it looks like our captain might be getting back together with his ex."

It felt like a punch to the gut. "Wh-what makes you say that?"

Chang smirked. "Garcia and I went over last night to get a picture of a cabin from Corrine Fleshman. As we were walking up her walkway, she was on his lap with her tongue down his throat. Her hands were all over him."

Blood drained from Genevieve's body. She couldn't breathe. Chang had to be lying. He just had to be.

"Can you believe that?" Chang scooted even closer, now his eyes were just inches from hers. She could smell his cologne. It practically choked her. "They were making out right in front of a window with the curtains pulled wide open. But they were married and have three kids together. Guess there isn't anything scandalous about that. Is there?"

Her stomach lurched. "Excuse me."

"Is something wrong?"

She pushed past him and ran to the bathroom. Chang's laughter followed her until the door closed behind her.

Mackey was washing her hands.

Genevieve rushed into a stall before the other woman would

have the chance to start talking. She sat on the seat and let the tears escape silently.

The water stopped, then Mackey's footsteps went toward the door. Once it closed behind her, Genevieve allowed herself to sob.

Why had she let herself fall for her boss? She'd been stupid to think it could work. Even worse, she'd given herself to him in the most personal way possible. And she'd been stupid enough to think it actually meant something.

What if she'd sent him straight into the arms of his ex-wife?

That was someone she stood no chance against—the mother of his children. They had three kids together, and one was now missing. He and Corrine shared something Genevieve could never share with him.

How was she ever going to face him again? He would eventually return to work—maybe soon if the lead on the cabin panned out. Then what? How could she ever look him in the eyes again? He would never respect her.

She would never be able to move through the ranks in this precinct. Or, if she did, she would always wonder if Nick pulled strings to keep her quiet about their night together.

What made all of this worse was the fact that his daughter was missing, abducted by a murderer, and all Genevieve could think about was her broken heart and potentially ruined career. She'd be the laughingstock of the station. Chang had already picked up on her feelings for Nick. How many others had too, but kept quiet about it?

Beyond all of this was Tinsley. The girl was fragile and had started to make friends with Nick's kids and Alex's daughter. She hadn't made any progress with any kids at school.

Now Genevieve wouldn't be able to take Tinsley on play dates anymore. She'd have to cut the girl off from the only kids she was starting to trust all because she'd slept with her boss.

One night of thinking with something other than her head, and she'd ruined her life and Tinsley's in fell swoop.

The door to the bathroom opened.

"Are you still in here, Foster?" Mackey asked.

Genevieve cleared her throat as quietly as possible. "Yes."

"Garcia wants you to join him and Chang. They're going out with the feds to look at the cabin."

She wiped her eyes. "Tell them I'll be right there."

"Okay." The door closed.

Genevieve lowered herself to the floor and vomited into the toilet.

BACK

Ava struggled against the ropes. Dave had tied her ankles and wrists, then wrapped more rope around her arms and knees. Now she was flat on her back on the uncomfortable bed with no way to break free. She couldn't even scream for help because he'd duct taped her mouth.

There was literally nothing she could do to get out. Part of her wished Zoey would come back to help her, but she was glad Zoey hadn't. There was no doubt in her mind that Dave would keep his word and shoot both of them.

Hopefully Zoey would be able to find her way out and bring help. Dave had basically left Ava there to waste away. She'd had nothing to eat or drink, and despite her best efforts, she'd peed herself about an hour earlier.

Something sounded not too far away.

Ava's heart jumped into her throat. Was that good news or bad? Had Zoey already found help and brought them? Or was it just Dave making noise?

She held her breath and listened, not able to hear much over the sound of her pulse drumming in her ears.

Breathe, just breathe.

That was easier said—thought—than done because of the duct tape and the dust that was irritating her nose.

Finally she calmed herself enough to actually listen.

It was a dull, repetitive sound.

What was he doing?

It finally hit her. Dave was snoring. The jerk was sleeping soundly enough to snore while Ava was struggling against the ropes and while Zoey was out in the woods, fighting to find her way out.

Anger surged through Ava and she struggled all the more against the ropes. Things looked as bleak as they could be, but she couldn't give up now.

She wouldn't.

There had to be something she could do. She just hadn't looked hard enough yet.

Ava took a deep breath through her nose and studied the room as best she could with the daylight coming through the closed, ripped curtains.

The room was still *mostly* bare, but not entirely. That meant she could find something to help her. Maybe something to cut against the ropes or a way out without waking Dave.

Something.

Anything.

It didn't matter what. She scanned the room. Then her gaze landed on a stray piece of wood. The edge looked rough enough to rub against the ropes and maybe be able to free herself.

She just needed to get to the ground without making a sound, then maneuver herself over to the wood and grab it from behind. Then she needed to be able to angle it just right to cut the ties.

It sounded impossible, but it was all she had.

She had to try. It beat the alternative.

Ava squirmed and threw her weight to move her closer to the bed's edge.

Squeak! Creak!

She held her breath and closed her eyes—like that would hide her from Dave if he heard her.

Silence.

Then a distant snore.

Ava breathed a sigh of relief. She squirmed and wiggled some more, inching closer to the edge of the bed.

It felt like it was taking forever. If only she had a button she could push. An app would be nice. Or even just not being there at all. That would be best. Dave would pay. She would make sure of that once she broke free of the ropes.

But that would mean reaching the floor first. That could take all year at the rate she was going.

She continued struggling. Inching. Trying to stay quiet while listening for him. All she heard was the occasional distant snore.

Then her arm brushed the edge of the bed!

Ava swung her feet over while holding her upper body weight over the bed. One wrong move and she would crash to the floor and undoubtedly wake Dave.

Her heart pounded.

Just a little farther.

Ava's toe brushed the floor. She pressed both feet down flat. Once she was sure she'd be able to hold her body weight, she pushed off against the bed and stood.

She stared at the wood. It felt light years away. But she'd made it this far. She could keep going and pick it up.

All she had to do was to keep her balance while making her way over, one little bit at a time.

She wiggled her fingers, readying them to grab the wood.

Something crashed in the next room.

CONVINCE

Alex sat at the edge of his bed. His head pounded and ached, but it was nothing compared to what it could've been if he'd given into temptation the night before.

With a fresh morning perspective, he was glad he hadn't. He was actually surprised he hadn't. He'd wanted a drink so bad.

It was no wonder people went to meetings and had sponsors. He wanted to call someone and talk about how great it felt to have faced temptation that had grabbed him by the throat and to have walked away without giving in.

But even so, there was no time for celebration. Not with Zoey and Ava missing.

Alex grabbed his phone and checked for any news updates. Nothing new, unfortunately.

There was a text from his mom asking if he needed anything and saying that Macy and the baby were back from the hospital. He sent a quick thanks, and said he didn't need anything.

A twinge of guilt pricked him for not visiting his sister and nephew in the hospital, but he'd been there for the birth. That counted for a lot more, didn't it?

What was everyone telling her about Zoey? Macy had to be

furious, or at least hurt, that her lifelong best friend hadn't been there for the biggest moment of her life.

Was it crueler to leave her wondering or to tell her the truth?

Alex called Luke, hoping he wasn't asleep.

"Hey, Alex." The new dad sounded tired.

"How's Macy and the baby? Sorry I didn't make it to the hospital."

Luke yawned. "Don't worry about it. You have your own stuff to deal with."

"Have you told Macy about Zoey?"

"I told her how sick Ariana is and led her to believe Zoey was sick, too. I just couldn't bring myself to tell her. Is that selfish? I hate keeping it from her."

"So do I, but it's for the best. She doesn't need that kind of stress right now."

"That's what I keep telling myself, but I know she's going to be mad at me when she finds out." Luke yawned again.

"Even if she is upset, she'll understand. She'll have all these memories untainted from everything else going on. Hey, did you guys pick a name yet?"

"We did. The hospital staff didn't want us leaving without one. Your nephew is Caden Alexander."

"What? Alexander?" If Alex wasn't already sitting, he would need to. "Not Lucas? Or your dad's name?"

"We both agreed you make a great namesake. You're going to be the cool uncle he looks up to. Besides, the two names have a good sound, don't you think?"

"Wow, thanks. I don't know what to say."

"You don't have to say anything." Luke yawned for the third time. "But if you don't mind, I'm going to see if I can get a little nap before Caden wakes again."

"Yeah, sure." They said quick goodbyes while Alex let the name sink in. He wasn't sure if it was because of Zoey's disappearance, but them picking his name left him with a lump in his throat.

He gave himself a minute to let it settle, then he called Nick.

"Alex, what's going on?" Nick's voice was thick and groggy.

"Sorry if I woke you."

"What time is it?"

"After ten."

Nick swore, and rustling noises sounded on the other end. "I should've set my alarm."

"Do you have somewhere to be?"

"I'm trying to figure out what to do about Corrine."

"What about her?"

He muttered something. "She's lost her mind."

"Ava's missing, I'm not surprised. We're all going a little crazy right now."

"No, I mean seriously, she's lost her mind. She's trying to win me back."

"Really? You think it's the stress of everything? Maybe she's just reaching out to what's familiar, and you guys were together forever."

"I had that thought too, but while I was unable to sleep last night another idea struck me. One that scares me to the core."

Alex's mind raced, trying to figure it out. "What is it?"

"Come over here. We'll talk over breakfast."

His stomach rumbled. "You don't have to ask twice."

Twenty minutes later, Alex sat at Nick's table, sipping too-strong coffee while his friend flipped bacon.

Nick still hadn't said anything about his idea. Alex wasn't going to press—not yet. If he didn't start talking once the food was gone, Alex would ask.

It only took a few minutes for the omelets and bacon to disappear, then Nick leaned back in his chair and took a deep breath.

Several beats of silence passed between them before Nick looked at Alex. "Corrine has taken me for a fool all this time."

Alex arched a brow but said nothing.

"She hid not only an affair from me—we were engaged, that counts as an affair, right?"

"Sure."

"But she also hid a baby from me! A baby! She was pregnant with another man's baby while we were together, then she took off as soon as she couldn't hide it from me. I never questioned a thing. Not once. I trusted her like a pathetic lovesick puppy."

Alex felt like he should say something to make Nick feel better, but he didn't want to interrupt, so he kept silent.

Nick tapped the table. "She still views me that way. To her, I'm nothing more than a pawn to get what she wants. Corrine always knew I'd make something of myself, and that would make her look good as my wife. She wanted a cushy life and kids. I gave her that. We were never rich but also never in need."

Alex nodded, trying to figure out where Nick was going.

"But no matter what I did, it was never enough. Do you know why?"

"No."

"Because she had another baby out there. A child she couldn't have a relationship with because she never told me about him. Nothing I could give her would make up for that."

"Does this have something to do with what's going on now?"

"I'm almost there. She's so used to pulling the wool over my eyes—our entire marriage was nothing other than a lie built on a foundation of deceit. Corrine thinks she can keep that up, and now she still has a secret, but this time it's bigger than before." Nick drew in a deep breath. "I think she's somehow involved with the shooting. Ava's abduction. The whole thing."

Alex stared at Nick, trying to make sense of his theory. "But she's freaked out over the whole thing, right?"

"She's afraid of being caught. Corrine has always been terrified of jail. I'm sure she's having second thoughts. She wants out but doesn't know how because she's in too deep. So, she either wants to bring me in as an accomplice or to protect her. Or she's trying to distract me, so I don't figure out the truth. She's dreaming, either way."

"Why don't you just turn her in?"

"On what? The fact that she has a kid with Dave? Sure, she hid that, but there's no *proof* that she's involved with this. The most we could get her for is questioning. Then she'll flee."

Alex's eyes widened. "But she'd go right to Dave. She'd lead the cops to him!"

Nick tapped the table and glanced out the window. "Maybe..."

"If she's really working with him, she would."

"But if not, I'd be the laughingstock of the force. Nobody would respect me anymore. I wouldn't respect me."

Alex shook his head. "You told me everything, and it hasn't changed how I think about you."

Nick frowned. "You're my friend."

"And just like everyone else, I know you. You're strong, have a good work ethic, and command respect. They're only going to think badly of her. That's it."

"If I'm going to turn her in, I need to have proof. But how am I going to get that?"

"Take her back."

Nick gave him a double-take.

"Pretend to want her back. She'll think you're under her spell. You can get her to spill the truth. And even if she won't, you'll be in her house. You can find the proof."

CABIN

Genevieve stared out the window from the backseat of the undercover car. She tried to ignore Garcia and Chang's conversation in the front seat as they drove the long stretch of highway with nothing other than trees to look at.

She didn't know why she was along with them. It would've made a lot more sense for her to ride with another officer—anyone other than Chang. Mackey would make a nice choice, but nobody else from the precinct was going with the feds to look at the cabin.

"You think the captain's going to get back together with Corrine?" Chang asked.

"Wouldn't surprise me," Garcia replied. "Stuff like this tends to bring people together or tear them apart."

Tears stung Genevieve's eyes. It was tearing her and Nick apart, and they'd only had the one night together. And worst of all, if he did return to his ex, she had no room to complain. Not when it could restore a family. Give three kids their parents back under one roof.

She felt like the most selfish person alive for wishing that would never happen. She was a horrible person.

"What do you think, Foster?" Chang asked. "Is our captain going to get remarried?"

She gritted her teeth. "I have no idea. Can we focus on the case?"

"This has everything to do with the case. Our captain is on leave because the person he used to bang is now banging our suspect."

"Would you grow up?" She glanced at Garcia, who didn't respond. "He's out because of his daughter, and you know it."

"That's part of it."

"No, that's all. Nick—I mean, the captain—needs to deal with that." Her face flamed at her mistake.

Chang glanced back and smirked.

Garcia didn't seem to notice the slip. He kept looking at the navigation unit. "We're almost there."

Genevieve relaxed. The sooner she was out of the car, the better. Chang would behave in front of the feds. She hoped.

Chang rattled on about the time when Nick had been married. He spoke of flowers sent and the blinds in his office being drawn numerous times when Corrine showed up at lunchtime. He glanced back. "What do you suppose they were doing in there? Taxes?"

She shot him a death glare. Unfortunately it didn't work.

Chang laughed. "I bet it involved cuffs. And maybe—"

"Shut up!" Her heart thundered and the tears threatened again. Both of them turned around and stared at her.

"I don't think this is a professional conversation."

Garcia nodded and turned back to the front. "Chang, help me find the turn-off. Half these road signs are covered by branches."

Genevieve drew in deep, silent breaths. If Chang was trying to make sure she'd be shaken up in front of the feds, it was working. She just wanted to curl up in the backseat and stay there. Not that it was an option, nor would she let anyone see that anything was wrong.

They finally turned off the main road and onto a rocky unmaintained path barely wide enough for a vehicle. Dozens of "No Trespassing" signs were posted, most riddled with bullet holes.

About half a mile down the way, they came to several unmarked cars parked in a tiny clearing. The cabin was nowhere in sight.

Garcia pulled off and parked next to a black SUV. He and Chang jumped out and started talking to the nearest federal agent.

Genevieve took her time unbuckling. She was still shaken from Chang's remarks. It was hard—no, impossible—not to let them get to her.

Usually, she could push any personal problem aside to do her job, but between everything with Nick and being back in a forest, it would take all her effort not to fall apart.

What had ever made her think she would make it as an officer of the law?

Chang tapped on her window. "Coming?"

She glared at him and stepped out.

One of the feds immediately gave instructions for how they were going to handle searching the cabin.

Everyone prepared. Genevieve, Garcia, and Chang were to check out the back of the building. Staying behind trees, everybody made their way to the cabin.

Once it came into view, Genevieve doubted it was the right place. The little building looked like it would crumble if someone sneezed near it. She stayed near Garcia as they crept around to the back.

Piles of rotting firewood went as far as they could see. It was the perfect place for hiding things—or people.

Her pulse raced as she approached the nearest one, gun drawn. Nothing was behind it. Or the next stack. In fact, there was nothing unusual near any of them.

Or the cabin itself. Some feds came out declared it not only clear, but untouched for years, covered in dust and cobwebs.

The lead agent shouted orders. He told Garcia to go back to Corrine's place and take her to the station for questioning.

"Come on." Garcia waved her and Chang in the direction of the cars.

Her stomach twisted. Another hour in the car with Chang, followed by having to be in the same room with him and Corrine.

HORRIFIED

Nick adjusted the bags over his shoulder before ringing the doorbell.

The curtain moved inside the window, and Hanna's little face appeared. Her expression lit up, then she disappeared.

The door flung open. "Daddy! I didn't know you were coming over again! What's in the bags?"

Nick gave her a quick kiss, then stepped inside.

Corrine appeared from the kitchen and arched a brow. "What's going on?"

"Like we talked about." Nick dropped his bags on the couch, making sure it was obvious they weren't going in her room. He needed to make it clear he would sleep on the couch. "We need to be together as a family right now."

"You're staying?" Hanna shrieked.

Parker appeared from down the hall. He didn't say anything.

Nick glanced back at Hanna and nodded. "I'm going to stay until we find Ava."

"Maybe longer." Corrine stepped closer. "I can take your bags."

"I'll sleep on the hide-a-bed."

Corrine frowned. "Are you sure?"

He nodded to keep himself from expressing just how vehemently sure he was. "It's for the best."

Hanna grabbed Nick's arm and dragged him down the hall. "Parker! Dad's staying with us!"

"Yeah, I heard." Neither his tone nor his expression indicated how he felt about it. "Why?"

"We all need to support each other. It'll be easier if we're all in the same house."

Parker folded his arms and the corners of his mouth curved down.

Nick put his arm around him. "You okay, buddy?"

Parker shrugged.

"If you have anything you want to say, say it. No judgments. Right?" He glanced over at Corrine.

"Of course not. Whatever you need to say is fine."

Parker stormed down the hall, went into his room, and slammed the door.

Nick's chest tightened. If pretending to move in was going to ruin the progress he'd made with his son, it wasn't worth it. He'd walk away in a heartbeat.

"Oh, he'll be fine." Corrine waved in his direction. "On top of everything else, he's hormonal. Puberty has struck."

"He's turning into a man," Hanna informed Nick.

"Let me talk to him."

Corrine intercepted him and wrapped her arms around him. "Parker just needs space. He's always been that way, and now more than ever."

Nick forced a smile, then stepped away from her hold. "Still, I think I should talk to him. I'm the one who just showed up without warning. I'm sure it's confusing."

Corrine glanced over at Hanna, who was now lounging on the couch, using one of Nick's bags as a pillow. "She seems fine."

"She also isn't Parker." Nick headed down the hall before Corrine could keep him any longer.

He twisted the knob, but it didn't budge.

"Go away!"

Nick leaned against the door. "Can we talk?"

"No! Leave me alone."

He took a deep breath. "Would you prefer I went back to my condo? I will, if you want me to."

Silence.

"Just say the word, and I'll leave."

Corrine threw him a pleading glance.

Nick tapped on the door. "Parker?"

Click.

He'd unlocked it. Maybe all wasn't lost.

Nick opened the door and slid inside. "Thanks for letting me in."

Parker shrugged. He sat with his back to Nick at his desk, facing the window.

"You want to talk about me coming here to stay with you guys?"

"What's there to talk about?"

Nick closed the door and sat on the bed across from his son. "Other than the fact that your mom and I are divorced, and I'm staying here for a little while?"

Parker turned to him and met his gaze. "Why? Are you getting back together? Or just trying to mess with me and Hanna when we're already having a hard enough time?"

"I'm definitely not messing with you two. I would never do that, ever. But with everything going on, your mom and I thought it would be better if I stayed here."

"How long?"

"Just until Ava comes back. I'm going to crash on the couch. I don't want you to get your hopes up."

"I don't *want* you guys getting back together."

Nick lifted a brow. "You don't?"

Parker shook his head. "You're both happier—and nicer—now."

"I wasn't nice before?"

Parker groaned. "You know what I mean."

"Actually, I don't."

"You guys don't really fight now. You let us do more. That sort of thing." He shrugged and looked out the window.

Nick tapped his knee. "None of that is going to change, kiddo. I'm just going to sleep on the couch and be here for you whenever you need me."

"Okay."

Nick studied his son, but reading him when he didn't want to be read was like trying to read a brick wall. "Is it okay with you if I stay here for a while?"

"You actually care what I think?"

Nick threw his head back. "Of course I do. That's why I'm in here talking to you."

"You didn't ask me what I thought before you showed up with your bags."

Nick took a deep breath. "You're right, I didn't. I just showed up, and I'm sure that threw you off. I'm sorry, Parker. I wasn't thinking about that. Just that your mom had invited me to stay here."

Parker turned back to him. "She did?"

Nick nodded.

"Huh." He turned back to his desk. "I have homework to do before I fall behind."

"Sounds good." Nick rose and rubbed Parker's shoulders for a moment. "If you want to talk about anything man-to-man, I'm here. You can wake me in the middle of the night if that's when you need me."

Parker turned around and smiled.

Nick's heart warmed and expanded. "I love you, kiddo."

"Love you too, Dad."

He squeezed Parker's shoulders again, breathed a silent sigh of relief, then went back into the hallway. Then he leaned against the wall and realized just how tired and tense he was. A hot shower was just what he needed.

Nick went into the bathroom and turned on the water. He found a towel, then climbed in and closed his eyes as the burning water ran down and soothed him. He stood there as time seemed to stand still. The water eventually cooled, then he soaped up with body wash in a Star Wars bottle and used shampoo that smelled like grapes. Definitely the kids' bathroom.

He rinsed off as the water was turning cold, then dried himself and wrapped the towel around his waist. It felt like forever since he'd felt so relaxed. Now all he needed was for Ava to be returned safely, then he would sleep for a week and life would be perfect.

Part of him didn't want to leave the bathroom, but he needed to get dressed and then see what he could learn from Corrine. She had to be involved. If she wasn't working with Dave, then she had to be hiding something. He must have contacted her—why else would he have taken Ava, if not to use her as a bargaining chip to get Corrine back?

Nick flung the door open and headed for his bags to grab his clothes. It wasn't until he reached the couch that it registered that he heard conversation.

Garcia, Chang, and Foster all stood in the living room, talking with Corrine. Nick's gaze locked with Foster's. The shock and hurt in her eyes cut him to the core.

Chang arched a brow and tilted his head. "Captain."

Foster pulled out her phone and looked at the screen. "I have to deal with this in the car." She raced for the door.

Nick reached out, but had to grab his towel as it was about to slip. "Wait, I—"

Foster was gone.

Nick's insides tensed. He grabbed both bags. "Excuse me."

In the bathroom, he threw them on the floor and swore under

his breath. He knew exactly what Genevieve was thinking, and he couldn't blame her. It couldn't have looked worse. Nick hadn't returned any of her calls or texts, then he comes out in a towel at his ex's house. He swore again and pulled on some clothes without paying any attention.

Then grabbed his cell phone and raced for the front door.

Everyone looked at him.

Nick turned the knob. "I need to get something from my car."

Chang gave him a look like he knew better.

Great.

EXPLAIN

Nick ran toward the unmarked police cruiser, his mind racing and his heart nearly exploding out of his chest.

Genevieve wasn't anywhere. He looked up and down the street, then he noticed movement in the back of the car.

He raced over and tapped on the window.

She was busy with her phone and didn't look up from the screen.

Nick tapped again, this time faster.

She still didn't move her gaze.

He pulled on the door handle. Locked. He knocked. "Foster!"

Nothing.

"Genevieve!"

She looked up.

"We need to talk!"

Genevieve shook her head. Her disappointed expression said more than enough.

"Please!" He pulled on the handle again.

She turned back to her phone.

Nick leaned against the front car door and raked his hands through his hair.

Chang was looking out through the living room window.

"My day is complete." Nick's mind raced, trying to figure out a way to get Genevieve out of the car so he could explain himself.

Then he thought of something.

Nick pulled out his phone. He called her.

One ring, then it went to voicemail.

He spun around and threw her a pleading look. She had her back to him, facing the other side of the vehicle.

Nick called again, but this time it went straight to voicemail.

He went over to their texting conversation.

That wasn't what it looked like. Let me explain.

If she got the message, she didn't respond—with a text or by turning around. That left him with only one option. He would have to explain himself through texts. The ball would then be in her court.

I'm only staying here on the couch to be here for the kids and to see if I can get a confession out of Corrine.

He waited for her to respond. She didn't.

I don't trust that she's telling us everything she knows. I'm playing good cop, that's it.

Genevieve didn't respond.

Nick's mind raced. What could he say to get her attention?

I'm really sorry I haven't gotten back to you. I've been meaning to. It's just that I'm barely functioning with Ava missing.

He waited, hoping that was what she wanted to hear. If it was, she still wouldn't look at him or text back.

I really appreciate you being there for me the other night.

Still nothing.

He waited longer before sending another text, hoping she'd at least glance his way.

I don't blame you for being pissed at me. I deserve it the way I treated you. I'm sorry.

No response.

If you hate me, it won't affect work. You're a good officer and I want to see you succeed. You don't have to worry about your career. Nothing has changed in that regard.

He glanced back.

She had her face in her palms.

It gutted him. He wanted to throw open the door and wrap his arms around her.

Garcia and Chang now stood on the front stoop, talking to Corrine.

Garcia and Chang are coming.

I really am sorry.

Without glancing back, Nick marched up the walkway with an air of confidence that was fully faked. He nodded to Garcia, who nodded back.

Chang, who had fallen behind the detective, stopped and made eye contact with Nick. "Did you get what you needed from your car?"

Nick drew his brows together. "I may be on leave, but don't forget who the captain is."

"And don't you forget there are rules in the force. This isn't a dictatorship."

"What exactly are you trying to say, Officer?"

Chang crossed his arms. "Hey, I get it. Foster's a hot little thing. Can't blame you. You're only human."

Nick clenched his fists and held them close to keep from hitting him. "What do you want?"

"Just to move through the ranks as quickly as I deserve. Nobody can keep a secret like I can—for friends."

Nick drew in a deep breath. So the officer was going for blackmail. There was no other choice but to go along with it since he already knew too much. Nick would go along with it for now. Once he had Ava back, he'd dig up some dirt on Chang and make him wish he'd never crossed his boss. "Fine."

"So we have an understanding?"

Nick nodded. "But leave Foster out of it. Your issue is with me. Got it?"

"Sure, no problem."

"I'm serious. If I find out you're giving her grief, I'm going to be pissed."

An odd expression crossed Chang's face. "Yeah, okay. Have a good day, Captain."

Nick glared at him. "You too."

They parted ways, and Nick headed back to the house. Chang was going to go down. How dare he blackmail Nick when his kid was missing?

ALONE

Z oey leaned against a tree and pulled another sliver of wood
from her foot. Blood oozed out, running over dirt and
crusted blood. Her feet ached and burned. But she barely noticed
it over the hunger and thirst.

She didn't know if she was moving closer to civilization or if
she was just going in circles. Everything looked different and
the same all at once. The only thing that gave her hope that she
was going the right way was that she hadn't come across
the cabin.

In fact, she hadn't come across any other signs of humanity.
She'd run into several wild animals, but nothing too scary.

Zoey slid down to sitting and closed her eyes. Exhaustion ran
through her in waves, and this time she didn't fight it. As much as
she just wanted out of the woods, she needed sleep. So far, she
hadn't allowed herself much, hoping to reach help.

Suddenly, it didn't seem to matter. She wouldn't even be able
to tell anyone where the cabin was. Though she had a good sense
of direction, the whole world was turned around at this point.

Her mind felt like it was floating above her. Alex and Ariana
appeared, playing a board game. They didn't see her. Zoey knew it

was a dream, but she still ran toward them, ready to embrace them.

Everything melted away around her before she could reach them.

Zoey woke with a start. She rubbed her eyes and looked around. It was dark now. How much time had passed? With as groggy and rested as she felt, it had to have been at least a couple hours.

Snap!

She froze. Her pulse pounded.

Snap!

Zoey scrambled to her feet, keeping her back pressed against the tree. She couldn't tell which direction the breaking twigs came from. Holding her breath, she waited.

A wild dog appeared in front of her. A coyote? A wolf? She didn't know the difference, but it didn't matter. What she needed was to get away.

It met her gaze and paced in front of her, not looking away.

Zoey's heart beat wildly out of control. If she ran, it would chase her. If she stayed where she was, it could attack her. It might be able to sense her fear. It was probably sending a silent call for the rest of its pack.

She swallowed, not looking away. Her pulse pounded even faster, though she didn't think that was possible.

The dog stopped pacing, then sat.

Was that good or bad? It wasn't growling. That had to be good. Unless it was just waiting for the rest of its family to arrive.

Zoey imagined a pack growling at her. The lunging, teeth ready to tear into her skin.

She hadn't come this far to be taken out by wild animals. No, she needed to get home to her family. Ava needed her to get help.

Even though Zoey didn't know exactly where the cabin was, she could at least give a general direction. The police could comb the area and find it.

She took a deep breath and licked her lips, not that it helped. Her tongue was just as dry as her chapped lips. Her hands shook and her knees wobbled.

Zoey took a small step forward. She held her breath, waiting for the dog to lunge for her.

It didn't budge.

She nearly threw up. "N-nice doggie."

Its tail twitched slightly.

"I-I'm just going to walk away. I w-won't hurt you."

The dog kept still.

Zoey took another step and waited.

It stayed where it was.

She looked around for others, hiding or approaching. There were none that she could see.

"I'm just going to walk away," she repeated.

The dog didn't move.

Zoey turned her head but kept it in the corner of her vision as she took one slow step after another until it was finally out of sight.

She wanted to burst into a run but kept her steps steady, listening for the sounds of the animal coming after her.

Everything remained silent. She continued walking, picking up her pace just slightly with each step. Rocks and sharp twigs dug into her feet but she was growing used to it.

Snap!

Zoey spun around, her throat closing.

The dog was trotting after her.

Trotting?

It caught up and looked at her, tilting its head.

Mind reeling, Zoey swallowed and continued walking. The dog caught up and walked next to her at the same pace.

Her pulse raced through her body, but she pretended not to notice the animal. She just kept going, moving a little faster. It did the same. She slowed. So did it, staying next to her.

DESPAIR

Alex stared at Nick's latest text and leaned against his couch. Nobody had been at the cabin. It had been a false lead. Not only that, but Nick hadn't gotten anything out of Corrine or found anything to implicate her.

They were back to square one with no clue where Dave had taken Zoey and Ava, or why. And it had been days. Days! In most cases, when a killer was bent on murder, it happened within hours.

That led to the question of whether Dave took them to kill them or for some other reason.

Alex dropped the phone into his lap and closed his eyes. Fatigue squeezed but wouldn't allow him any rest. The moment he tried to sleep, bloody images filled his mind, making staying awake preferable.

He knew what would help him relax.

Not this again.

No! Alex wasn't going to give in. He'd already made up his mind. Temptation had been beat the moment he stepped away from the alcohol aisle.

But here he was again. The drink was calling his name. Singing the song he had given into for far too long. It was stronger than that of the mythical siren.

No. He had to resist. It wasn't just one drink. It was never just one. He could fall asleep without it.

Alex closed his eyes, determined to sleep. Once again, images of Zoey's battered and bloody body taunted him.

What if she really was already dead? Statistically, she was. But Alex knew statistics weren't always right.

But what if they were this time? He'd been lucky so many times before. Luck could only last so long. What if he'd run out?

He'd been stupid to lose Zoey in the first place. Then even more so to keep pushing her away all those years. He'd probably even been an idiot for waiting so long to propose.

Now what? Had he lost his one true love forever?

Was it just his destiny to never fully have the woman of his dreams? Everything had been against them from the very beginning. Zoey had been fifteen when he was thirteen. She'd also been his sister's best friend. Then Macy went missing just after they'd admitted their true feelings to each other. Then came Ariana at such a young age. They'd weathered that, but stuff had always led to a rocky relationship until they finally broke up and went their separate ways.

Alex sat up and banged his fist on the coffee table. He swore at the unfairness of it all.

Sure, he deserved all the heartache, but she didn't. Just look at all the pain he'd inflicted on her. Teenage pregnancy. Breaking up with her the way he had. Hell, even Ariana's abduction was his fault. Had he been watching her like he should have, she'd have never followed Flynn out of the Ball Palace. Now Alex couldn't find Zoey. Everything bad was his own damn fault.

Alex hit the table again. He really did need a drink.

His mouth watered and his insides pressed on him, both inward and outward.

Just one drink. That's all he would need to relax and get some decent sleep. It wasn't like he was going to drink to get drunk. Just to rest. So he could focus on finding more clues online. He couldn't focus when he was this tired.

If he had just one beer, it would be a *service* to everyone. He would be a hero, really. All he needed to do was to find the one missing clue that had to be just out of his reach.

And to do that, he needed sleep. To sleep, he needed one beer. Just one. All he had to do was go to the store. Then everything would be fine. Zoey would be in his arms. Ava would be in Nick's. Dave would be in jail.

Alex grabbed his phone, shoved it into his pocket, found his keys, and headed for the door. Relief washed through him, just having made the decision.

CONFUSION

G enevieve clutched her phone and pressed her head against the headrest. She stared at the maple tree just outside her car as if it could give her answers.

As soon as Garcia had pulled into the parking lot at the station, she had fled without a word to her car. Despite the hours that had passed, she hadn't moved. She'd watched the sun go down behind the tree.

She wanted to reread Nick's texts but was afraid they would hurt too much. More than anything, she wanted to believe everything was true, but Chang's words kept echoing through her mind. She didn't want to be the person that kept three kids from having their parents together.

A text came in. She swung the screen in front of her, hoping it was Nick, then hating herself for wanting it so bad.

It was from her parents, wanting to know if they should put Tinsley to bed at their place.

Tinsley. She'd completely forgotten. Some foster parent she was.

Does Tinsley want me to come get her?
It's hard to tell.

Of course. Because the traumatized girl only spoke to Genevieve.

I'll be right there. Sorry.

She hurried to her parents' house. Tinsley lay on the couch, watching a cartoon. Genevieve went over and sat next to her feet. "You ready to go home?"

The girl turned to her and half-smiled.

"Today was rough at work. I hope you had a better day than me."

Tinsley gave her a slight nod.

"Good. Should we get home?"

She got up and put her shoes on.

Genevieve exchanged a look with her parents. If only she knew how to get her to open up, but even the therapist—the expert of childhood trauma—could only do so much. And Genevieve was no expert. She certainly wasn't a parent, but she was trying.

She got up and patted Tinsley's shoulder. "I don't know about you, but I could use some ice cream."

"Bye, Tinsley." Genevieve's mom gave her a big smile, then turned to Genevieve. "I'm off again tomorrow if you need me to watch her. Do you know when the kids are going back to school?"

"I haven't heard, but they're still getting homework. They have to figure out where all those kids are going to go, and there's so much of the building destroyed. They're talking about possibly starting over from the ground up. If that's the case, they'll have to move the kids around to other local schools."

Tinsley stared at her, but of course didn't say anything. It was nothing short of a miracle she hadn't been there the day of the shooting.

Genevieve patted her back. "Nothing to worry about. It'll get figured out."

They said their goodbyes and headed home. All of Genevieve's muscles ached and her head pounded. She was trying to ignore the worst pain of all—her heart.

Bowls of ice cream covered in chocolate sauce and sprinkles did help somewhat. Keeping the conversation going on her own at least kept her distracted until Tinsley went to bed.

Then she was left with her thoughts. She tossed and turned in bed, and then it felt like no time passed between falling asleep and the alarm going off.

She dragged herself out of bed and into the shower. Still bleary-eyed, she fixed some breakfast and dropped Tinsley back off at her parents' house.

Her mom welcomed Tinsley with a big smile. "I was thinking we could work on the garden today. You seemed interested in it yesterday. What do you think?"

Tinsley's eyes lit up and she nodded.

"You two have fun." Genevieve forced a smile, then headed to the station. Her stomach churned acid at the thought of having to face Chang for another day. She picked up a strong coffee on her way in.

To her surprise, he didn't bother her. Didn't even look up as she passed his desk on the way to hers. Was it another mind game? Just trying to make her worry about what was coming next?

There was no way he would stop torturing her about Nick, especially after he walked out in a towel, obviously not expecting to see anyone from work there.

Her breath caught as she remembered how good he had looked, but then her stomach knotted when she thought of what might've happened before she'd arrived.

She was a fool, and Chang knew it. He was going to hold it over her head until when? Until Genevieve moved to a different precinct? Or would he get bored and find someone else to bother?

"Here."

She looked up to see Chang standing about a foot away from

her desk, holding out a case file. She took it, and he left without a word.

Weird.

Genevieve watched him walk back to his desk and turn to his laptop. She glanced through the file. It was on the current case, their recent visit to Corrine's in particular, and needed her signature on some of the forms.

She filled it out and returned it to Chang, who took it back without a word. In fact, he barely looked at her. No smirking or hurtful comments.

"What's going on?" Genevieve demanded.

"Nothing." He typed on the keyboard, not looking away from the screen.

"You're not acting like yourself."

He kept his attention on the computer. "I'm just working. If you don't have anything to say about the case, I need to focus on this."

"Okay."

Later, Mackey invited her out to lunch. "A bunch of us are going to try that new Italian place. It's supposed to be good."

"Sure." Genevieve gathered her purse and rode with some others, including Chang. He didn't so much as look at her in the car or the restaurant. No sideways glances or comments.

It was nice, but she couldn't help worrying about what he had coming next.

REGRET

Alex woke to a blinding light. No, that was just the morning sun. He pulled the blankets over his face and groaned. His head felt like it had been run over by a truck. Actually, his entire body felt that way. His stomach wasn't doing so hot, either.

He tried to remember what would've caused this, but nothing came. Obviously, he was torn about Zoey. Worst of all was how fast the days were passing. He had no clue what day it was but it felt like she'd been gone longer than anyone else he'd had a hand in helping return home. Well, except his sister. She'd been gone for months. How had his parents survived that?

Alex needed to talk to Nick. Hopefully he'd found something from Corrine or her house. A clue that would lead them to Dave with Ava and Zoey.

He felt around for his phone, then pulled off the blankets slowly. The light still felt like razors to his eyes. What he needed was some ibuprofen, and quick. He covered his face with one arm and stepped out of bed.

His foot rolled over what felt like a glass bottle. Alex swung his arms out to regain his balance, blinding himself with the light again. He closed the curtains and squinted, glancing around.

Several empty beer bottles lay scattered around the bedroom. His heart sank.

He'd given in, and badly from the looks of it. How far had he gone? What had he done?

Alex held onto the wall as he crept out into the living room.

The first thing he noticed was more scattered, empty beer bottles. There were at least six, and he hadn't yet seen the kitchen or the other side of the couch. He could only see the back from where he stood. Who knew what lay in front of it, where he had probably crashed and watched the news, torturing himself.

The second thing he saw made his heart skip a beat.

Women's clothing.

No!

Black leggings, a pink shirt, socks, a bra, and panties trailed from the hallway to where he stood in front of his room.

No, no, no, no!

Alex leaned against the wall and covered his face. He hadn't— he couldn't have. No matter how desperate or in pain he was. Cheating on Zoey would ruin everything!

What had he done?

There was no undoing this. None at all. While his fiancée was fighting for her life, Alex had done the unthinkable.

He ran to the bathroom and retched in the toilet. Again and again until there was nothing left.

How could he do this? How could he be so stupid?

Why couldn't he have held himself together? Zoey would never forgive him. How could he blame her, when he would never be able to forgive himself either?

In one foolish, weak moment he'd manage to ruin the dreams of his daughter and fiancée. All three of them were so excited for the day Alex and Zoey would marry.

Now that would never happen.

He rose and cleaned himself up in the sink. His reflection showed a pathetic man. Alex balled his fist and punched the mirror. It cracked, spreading out in all directions. Blood and flesh stuck to the middle. Pain seared through his fingers, but he didn't care.

What he needed to do was to get the woman out of his apartment and then figure out what to do next. As tempting as it was to hide his mistake, he had to tell Zoey. Their relationship was based on truth.

He would have to explain that it was the drink that did this. He couldn't even remember any of it—not even leaving the apartment.

Alex stared at his fractured reflection. He didn't deserve Zoey, not before this screw-up, and definitely not after. And how was he going to explain the breakup to Ariana?

Tears blurred his vision. He was tempted to hit the mirror again with his remaining good fist, but it wouldn't hurt himself enough. What he needed was to have someone beat the crap out of him.

He glared at himself and released a string of profanities, calling himself the worst, most derogatory things he could think of. Still, it was too good for him.

His head continued to pound. Alex dug out some painkillers and swallowed a few. He needed to pull himself together to face the woman and kick her out.

After taking a few deep breaths, he locked the door and started the shower. That would buy him some time for the ibuprofen to kick in. He turned the water as high as he could stand it, preferring physical pain to emotional. Whether Zoey returned alive or not, his life was over. Either way, they weren't getting married. They would never be a family with Ariana. They'd never give her little brothers or sisters. All his dreams were dead. Gone. Destroyed. All because he was too stupid to live.

Why had he allowed himself to get his hopes up? To think he had a future with Zoey? He should have known he'd do something to screw it up. He was Alex Mercer, after all. Lifetime mess-up. The guy who would never get it all together.

What made him think he could pull off a career as a cop and be a husband to the most beautiful woman alive? Of *course* he would destroy it. That was what he did. Mess up everything he touched. Kind of like that guy who turned everything to gold, except that Alex turned everything to crap.

Eventually, the water turned cold. He stood there until he couldn't stand it. Then he dried off and tip-toed back to his room so as not to wake the woman before he was ready to talk to her.

Once dressed, he took a deep breath. It would be hard not to scream and kick her out, but she hadn't done anything wrong. Alex was pissed at himself. He couldn't take it out on whoever it was.

His heart raced as he crept toward the couch. What if it was someone he knew? That would make this horrible situation all the worse.

He froze when he saw the couch. It was empty.

Where was she? It wasn't a big apartment, and she hadn't been in the bedroom or bathroom. She wouldn't have gone anywhere without her clothes, which were still spread out on the floor.

Alex scanned every inch of the living room. She wasn't there. He went into the kitchen. Empty. He went back to the bedroom, even checking in the closet and under the bed.

The little one-bedroom apartment was empty.

He went back to the living room. "Hello? Are you still here?"

Nothing.

Alex drew in a deep breath, trying to make sense of it. Had the woman left in other clothes? Taken something of his? Or brought an overnight bag and just forgotten the stuff lying on the floor?

An overnight bag.

He slapped his forehead and ran over to the clothes. Stuffed under a side table was a gray bag with ZC embroidered across it.

It was Zoey's bag. She'd left it at his place just in case she needed it.

Alex ran over to it and picked it up. It was empty. The clothes strewn across his floor were hers. Not some random woman. He hadn't been unfaithful to Zoey!

He couldn't be sure why he'd taken out her clothes, but relief washed through him as he realized that was exactly what had happened. Maybe it had somehow made him feel close to her.

He picked up the clothes, held the shirt to his face and breathed in. It smelled like a mixture of her perfume and fabric softener. He closed his eyes and held the scent, imagining she was right there.

That had to have been what he'd done the night before.

HIDDEN

Nick jumped at the sound of a car door slamming outside. It was too soon for Corrine to be back. She'd taken the kids swimming to get their minds off everything, then they were going to the grocery store.

He tiptoed out of her room and peeked out the front window, anyway. A neighbor across the street pulled out of his driveway.

Nick breathed a sigh of relief and went back to the bedroom. So far, all he'd found were pictures of her oldest child tucked away in a wooden box. None of them gave Nick any clues. They spanned the boy's lifetime, so she'd either been collecting them over the years or Dave gave them to her when she lived across the country.

Not that it mattered, because none of it brought Nick closer to his daughter. She was still missing, and if Corrine knew anything, it wasn't in the box of photos.

He tucked it back underneath her bed, exactly as it had been placed. Next, he pulled out a shoe box. The perfect hiding spot. In his job, many revealing clues had been found in those.

Nick held his breath as he pulled off the top. Letters. Some in envelopes, others just folded paper. He grabbed one from the top and unfolded it. He recognized the handwriting immediately.

It was an old love letter from when they were dating. If only he could go back in time and smack some sense into his younger self. But then again, if he could, he wouldn't have his three kids—his reason for waking up every morning.

He set his old letter aside and picked up another. It was also from him, declaring his undying love for the cheater.

He decided to try an envelope next. It was written in a man's script, addressed to Corrine. No name, but an address from Connecticut. Nick opened it and regretted it. It was a love letter from Dave, written around the time Nick had written his.

How could he have been so stupid? Blinded by love—the expression couldn't have been more apt. That was a mistake he wasn't going to make again.

Nick picked up another envelope. Same handwriting, different address. This time North Carolina. The next one was from Florida, and the next from DC.

Was that because Dave had been working for the airlines all along, or because he moved often? Someone deranged enough to shoot up a school would have a hard time keeping relationships. It made sense that he'd move a lot.

Based on the dates, the man had sent Nick's wife letters all throughout their marriage. Most talked about their son, more than a few begged her to return to them.

Anger churned in Nick's gut. How had he missed the signs? He studied the envelopes for clues.

Then he noticed something. All of the letters were addressed to Corrine at a post office box one town over.

Sneaky little devil. She'd not only hid a child from him, but an entire relationship. Even if it had been one way. Dave's letters indicated that he hadn't been getting the response he'd wanted from her.

Nick was about to put the box away when one envelope

caught his attention. Its return address was from Washington state. He recognized the city name, but couldn't place it.

A car door slammed shut outside.

Nick jumped, then shook his head at himself for being so jumpy. He wasn't the one in the wrong. Corrine was.

Laughter sounded outside. It sounded close.

Like Parker and Hanna.

The key jiggled in the door.

Nick shoved the lid back on the box, pushed it back to its place under the bed, and jammed the envelope in his back pocket before leaping out of the room.

The door opened, and the kids' discussion grew louder.

Nick darted into the bathroom and took a deep breath. Had he lost track of time, or had they returned sooner than he'd expected?

Knock, knock!

"You in there, Daddy?" Hanna asked.

"Yeah, honey. I'll be out in a minute."

"Okay." Her footsteps faded away.

Nick closed his eyes and geared himself up for acting normal. He caught sight of himself in the mirror and noticed the envelope sticking out of his pocket.

Where could he hide it without folding it? Corrine would notice a new crease once he replaced it. She always noticed small details like that.

He held it up, trying to figure out what to do. Then he noticed something he hadn't before. The date stamp.

It was recent. As in, the last week. Just before the shooting.

Nick's heart nearly exploded out of his chest.

What was written in there?

Hands shaking, he pulled out the note. He read it slowly, having a hard time taking in the words.

Dave was begging Corrine to come back to them. He said that

would be his last letter, and if he didn't hear back by the day before the shooting, Corrine would regret it.

And she'd told nobody about that?

Fury tore through him. This letter could have saved Ava days ago! Days!

How could Corrine be so selfish and stupid? It was one thing to keep an affair from her husband, but to hide it to the detriment of their daughter?

Nick nearly ripped the hinges off the door as he flung it open.

"Parker! Hanna! You two need to go next door. Now!"

Hanna stared at him with wide eyes. "What—?"

"I said now!"

Corrine glared at him. "What are you doing, Nick?"

He held up the envelope. "We have to talk."

Her face paled. "What? How did you get that?"

Nick met Parker's gaze. "Take your sister next door, son. Now."

Parker scrambled from the couch, took Hanna's hand, then led her outside.

Nick waited until they had crossed the yard before he turned to Corrine. "You knew about this before it happened?"

"I didn't know he was going to do *that*!" She reached for the letter.

He pulled it back. "You had your chance to do something with this."

She jumped toward him, reaching around back. "You had no right to go through my things! Give it back!"

"Why? Because it makes you look guilty?"

"I'm not! The only thing I did was ignore him. I didn't want that psycho around."

"You withheld evidence from the police! Evidence that could've helped save our daughter. If anything has happened to her, just know that you're to blame!"

She shook her head.

He pointed to the return address. "Where is this? Is that his cabin?"

"I don't know." She reached for it again.

"Guess we'll find out." Nick pulled out his phone and called Garcia.

ASSAULT

Zoey froze mid-step. Her breath hitched and a chill ran through her. Tiny hairs rose on her neck and arms.

The dog stopped and turned, looking around. Its ears arched, and it released a low growl.

It could sense whatever Zoey could. If only she knew what it was.

The dog continued growling, focused behind Zoey.

A chill ran down her back, making her feel like someone was watching. It was so strong, she was certain someone—or something—was nearby.

Whether she ran or stayed, it was a risk. She could potentially run right to the danger since she didn't know where they were.

"Is someone there?"

Silence. Not even the dog growled.

Zoey couldn't risk being caught by Dave again.

Without putting another second's thought into it, she burst into a run, ignoring her already-sore feet as more sharp objects dug into them.

Footsteps sounded behind her. Hopefully it was just the dog.

Her heart threatened to explode out of her chest. She couldn't hear anything over the sounds of it and her harried breathing.

She glanced from side to side, still not seeing anything. It would be too hard to see something hiding in the woods as she ran.

The dog caught up with her and ran ahead, growling again.

It still felt like someone was watching. Chasing. Growing closer.

Everything ached. It didn't feel like she could go on, but there was no other choice. If she wanted to see her loved ones again, she had to keep going until she physically couldn't.

She pictured a road just out of sight. A road with cars full of people who would stop to help her. People who would call the cops and send help for Ava.

Zoey gasped for air, her mouth uncomfortably dry. Her calves burned. Sharp pains radiated out from her right knee.

Her left foot landed on a rock. It rolled out. She stumbled.

Almost fell. Caught her balance with her other leg.

Explosive pain shot out from her ankle. Everything else disappeared from her vision. Time seemed to move slower.

She gasped for air and felt her ankle. It felt normal to her hand's touch, but hurt inside.

Grimacing, she took a step. More pain.

Tears stung her eyes.

Snap!

Zoey glanced to the left. She couldn't see anything out of the ordinary.

Snap!

The dog whined, urging her to move.

Her ankle was hurting worse by the moment. The pain was growing hotter. Beads of sweat broke out on her forehead.

She gasped for air. There was no time to let an injury slow her. Not if she was going to see Ariana and Alex again.

Surely, they were fighting for her.

She had to fight, too.

And she would.

Zoey pressed her foot down, putting weight on the screaming ankle. It held her weight.

She burst into a run again. It was awkward and wobbly, but she was moving. Running from the danger and to her family.

Nothing would keep her from them. Not Dave, not the woods, not a wild animal.

The dog kept close to her, staying on her left side. The injured side. How did it know?

Gratitude ran through Zoey. With the dog at her side, she would make it.

She focused on the dog, on her family, on everything other than the ankle threatening to slow her down.

There was probably nobody behind her, anyway. She'd zigged and zagged through the forest and was now far from the cabin.

She hoped. There was the chance that she'd only gone in circles. It was so confusing.

Something hit her from the side and bounced off.

Zoey rubbed her arm. Blood dripped down, getting on her hand.

Something else hit her shoulder. A rock.

She ran away from the direction it had come.

Footsteps.

Someone slammed into her back, knocking her to the ground. Her chin hit an exposed root. She scrambled up to her knees, but her leg went out from under her.

Fingers wrapped around her throbbing ankle. "Thought you could get away, did you?"

Dave.

Zoey yanked her leg, but Dave clung to it.

The dog growled and snapped.

"Help me!" Zoey cried.

"Shut up!" He pulled on her leg, making her lose her balance.

Her chest crashed to the ground, and her head barely missed a rock sticking out from the dirt. She flipped herself over and kicked her legs to get away from him.

The dog lunged at Dave. He shoved it, and the dog yelped as it crashed into a tree. It regained its footing and raced at Dave, digging its teeth into his arm.

He grabbed the dog by its leg and threw it against the same tree. The poor thing howled and struggled to get up.

Zoey punched Dave in the face. "How dare you hurt an innocent dog?"

He shoved her and glowered at her. "Innocent? That thing bit me! And then you punched me. You're going to pay."

She kicked him in the groin.

His eyes widened and he let go.

Zoey scrambled to her feet. She'd gotten away before, she could do it again.

Dave shouted. It was a wordless sound, and primal.

It struck fear into her core.

Her head yanked back as he pulled on her hair. Before she realized what was happening, Dave had pinned her against him.

She squirmed to get out of his hold, and as soon as she realized that was futile, she kicked and elbowed him as hard as she could.

"I should've killed you when I had the chance."

A cold terror ran through her.

He dragged her behind a bush and shoved her against a tree. Her head struck with a painful thump. He held her into place, digging her flesh into the bumpy bark, and glowered at her. He was so close she could feel his hot breath on her face. "I'm really going to enjoy this."

Zoey screamed as loud as she could.

He covered her mouth.

She bit into his flesh, drawing blood.

Dave swore and shook out his hand, then he hit her across the face and called her several vulgar names.

She spit in his eye and darted out of his grasp.

His hands grasped her arms, his fingers squeezing hard enough to bruise. He threw her to the ground and straddled her. "I'm going to treat you like the piece of trash you are, then leave you here to rot in your regret."

PURSUE

Genevieve's headache wouldn't give up. The pain started in her temples and radiated out, making it nearly impossible to think. She was about to tell Garcia she needed to go home, when Anderson whistled and called everyone to the meeting room.

So much for going home. Everyone would probably be staying late. She grabbed two ibuprofen and downed them with room temperature coffee before heading to the meeting room.

Detectives Anderson and Garcia were looking at a tablet in the front of the room. Behind them, all the whiteboards were filled with information on the case.

All the seats were taken, so Genevieve leaned against the wall and tried to ignore her aching head. It was starting to squeeze and throb. Hopefully the medicine would kick in soon.

Chang raced into the room, then after looking around, stood next to Genevieve. She braced herself for a rude comment, but he just pulled out his phone, looking ready to take notes. Like she should've been. She grabbed her phone and found the notes app.

Garcia and Anderson told them about a cabin that they believed Dave Cooper was likely holding his victims. They had a recent letter addressed from there, and the police had missed it before because Dave's stepfather owned it. He had a different last name from Dave and it had never come up as one of Dave's previous residences.

Genevieve made note of everything as quickly as she could. Her head hurt worse than before but she ignored it. There was no other option.

Once the meeting was over, everyone spread out through the building, heading in different directions. Genevieve was once again paired with Garcia and Chang.

She gathered her things and headed out to the parking lot for the unmarked vehicle they'd used before. Before she made it outside, she froze.

Nick rounded the corner with his ex-wife.

It felt like a slap in the face.

"Come on," Garcia snapped.

She pulled her attention away from Nick and followed the detective outside. Between her pounding head and the shock of seeing Nick at the station with Corrine, it wasn't until they were halfway to the woods that she realized Chang still hadn't given her any cutting jabs. Maybe he hadn't seen Nick and his ex arrive at the station. That was the only explanation.

Her mind raced. If they were really about to bring Ava home, Nick would return to work soon. There was no way she could face him every day, if at all. Especially with him being the boss. She wouldn't be able to hide her emotions, and after their night together, her feelings had only grown—despite her efforts to squash them.

Once the whole mess was over, she would need to move to a different station. There was no other alternative. That way she wouldn't have to worry about facing him, and it would be a hundred times harder if he got back together with Corrine.

"Almost there." Garcia's voice brought her back to the present.

As they neared, more official vehicles came into view. Other than their force, there were feds and other precincts. If Dave was in fact at the cabin, there was no way he would escape. There looked to be enough law enforcement to surround a cabin four times over.

Hopefully this wasn't a false lead like the last time. Given how long Dave had been holding Ava and Zoey, their chances of survival were bleak. Because of that, she was glad Nick wasn't out with them—even if it meant he was with his ex-wife. At least they would have each other to lean on if something had happened to their daughter.

Her heart ached worse than her head at that thought, but she had to accept the situation for what it was. If the abduction led to a family being restored, she needed to be happy for them. That was the right thing to do, as much as it would hurt.

Up ahead, some cars turned off the main road. Other official vehicles followed.

Garcia tapped the steering wheel. "We're getting close. It's time to take down that bastard."

Chang nodded. "We're going to get him this time. I can feel it."

Genevieve leaned forward as best she could with the seatbelt across her chest and studied the scene in front of them. Her heart raced. This might really be it. Their chance to take down the school shooter and bring home Ava and Zoey.

Garcia turned on the blinker, then turned after the other cars in front. They came to a rough gravel road with plenty of deep potholes.

Chang rubbed his neck. "Nothing says 'go away' quite like whiplash."

For once, Genevieve had to agree with him. The horribly bumpy path made her think they were really on the right trail this time.

Garcia pulled off into a clearing along with the others. One of the federal agents was giving directions. Canine units and cadaver dogs were both sniffing around.

Genevieve's stomach lurched at the thought of the cadaver dogs finding anything. She knew the victims—maybe it hadn't been a good idea for her to be on the case, after all. She'd thought she could handle it since she wasn't close to either one.

Now she was here, so there was no going back. It was time to think about them as the victims and not of their first names, of people she sometimes hung out with socially so Tinsley could have more time with other kids.

"One of the cadaver dogs smells something!"

She spun in the direction of the voice. Several officers and two dogs were heading deeper into the woods.

Genevieve closed her eyes. Just because they smell something didn't mean it was Ava or Zoey—the victims she was here to save.

A minute later, everyone started creeping toward the cabin. It didn't come into sight right away. Genevieve started to worry they weren't in the right place until the small building finally came into view.

Everyone took position behind trees, guns ready, all around the cabin. Genevieve craned her neck to see what she could. The only window in view was covered from the inside. If there were any lights on inside, they were well hidden.

Some of the feds charged toward the building without a sound.

Genevieve's heart beat so hard she could feel it through her entire body. She took deep breaths and pretended she wasn't in the middle of a forest. Maybe what she needed was to look into other departments that didn't hunt criminals in the woods. Maybe a city instead of a small town.

Bang!

A gun had been fired toward the cabin.

Bang! Bang! Bang!

Genevieve readied her gun and waited for permission to charge.

Everyone remained in their places.

Footsteps and shouting thundered from the other side of the building. More gunfire.

A girl screamed.

Genevieve's stomach lurched. She clenched her jaw, hoping that would be enough to keep her food down. No way she was going to vomit and show weakness around her brothers and sisters in blue. Being a woman put her at a disadvantage to begin with, despite how equal everything was supposed to be. She wasn't going to add to that by throwing up in front of anyone.

More screaming. Shots fired. Glass shattered.

Garcia gestured to head toward the building. Genevieve and several others followed. They stepped out of the shadows and toward the noise.

Once on the other side of the house, Dave—she recognized him from the pictures—held Ava in front of him and had a gun to her head. She was wrapped in ropes and tears ran down her face.

Nothing good ever happened in the woods.

She shoved those thoughts from her mind. The only thing that mattered was getting Ava from him alive.

RACING

Alex called Nick. Again. Social media and the news was buzzing that the police were hot on Dave's trail, but there were no details. Just rumors and guesses—nothing more than theories.

Voicemail.

He ended the call and tried again. Nick would either block him or answer. Alex wasn't going to leave him another choice.

On the fourth ring, Nick answered. "I'm a little busy, Alex!"

"Did they find Dave? Are Zoey and Ava with him?"

"I don't know if they've found him, but there's a good chance they will, if they haven't already."

"What's going on?"

"I found an address in Corrine's things. It belongs to Dave's stepdad who has Alzheimer's. He doesn't remember the cabin or Dave."

The room spun around Alex. He stumbled to the couch and sat. "So, the cops really are on their way to them?"

"If they're still there. The last lead was disappointing. I'm trying not to get my hopes up."

Shouting sounded in the background.

"Where are you?" Alex asked.

"At the station. Corrine was so upset she couldn't drive, so I had to." He took a deep breath.

"Is she involved?"

"No, and unfortunately, the only thing she's guilty of is stupidity. She withheld evidence that could've helped the case along earlier."

"What? Are you kidding me?"

"Nope."

"Well, can't she get in trouble for hiding evidence?"

"Yeah, and she probably will, though it won't be more than a slap on the wrist."

"For real?" Alex jumped up and paced. "She could've saved everyone a lot of time and grief!"

"I know, but now that she's cooperating..." Nick's voice trailed off.

"Not that she would have if you hadn't found the address." Alex wanted to hit something but instead rubbed his sore knuckles. He was probably lucky he hadn't broken any bones on the mirror. No sense in tempting fate a second time. "So, what's the address?"

"Why? You planning on heading out there?"

"If Zoey's there, yeah."

"They'll have to send her to a hospital to be looked over. You know how that goes."

Alex drew a deep breath. "I want to be there to see her with my own eyes. To hold her close."

"You think I don't want the same for Ava? I want to wrap my arms around her and never let go. But I'm going to follow protocol and wait."

"Will you at least tell me the general location so I can head for the nearest hospital?"

Nick muttered something Alex couldn't make out, then told Alex the name of a hospital.

Alex looked it up on his phone. It was just over two hours

away. He could make it in one hour. "Thanks. Will you let me know if anything else comes up? Just a text will do."

"Yeah, I'll try to remember."

"Try?"

"I'm under as much stress as you! All any of us can do is the best we can. I can't make any promises."

"Understood. Thanks again." Alex ended the call, gathered what he needed for the drive, and headed out.

He turned on his radar detector and peeled out of the parking lot. With any luck, he would be close enough to the cabin to be able to see Zoey before they carted her off to the hospital.

Alex shuddered, thinking of the shape she was probably in after being held captive. He refused to let himself think she was anything other than okay.

He tried to think of other things as he drove, but his mind kept wandering back to her and Ava. Then to Corrine. It made no sense that Dave hadn't sent any ransom notes to her. He wanted her back and had her daughter—he had to have contacted her. It just didn't make any sense that they wouldn't be in contact.

And that made Alex's blood boil. If she could've put a stop to the hostage situation but hadn't...

He gripped the steering wheel, making his knuckles turn white. Ava and Zoey didn't deserve any of this.

Why hadn't he just taken Corrine? That was who he had wanted. Killing people and holding others hostage was completely unnecessary.

As Alex drove along now on the winding road surrounded by woods, his anger growing, he hoped he would find Dave before the police. Give him a little vigilante justice and call it self-defense.

He checked the radar detector, then pressed harder on the gas. Though this was a different highway altogether, it reminded him of the one he'd taken not that long ago on his way to what should've been his first day of the police academy.

Chills ran down his back at the thought of it. The people who had hurt him were dead or in jail. Soon Dave would suffer the same fate.

Though Alex would've loved nothing more than to get his hands on him, it gave him comfort that there would be no way he would escape the death penalty. Not after everything he'd done.

A gray and white dog ran out in front of the car. Alex slammed on his brakes. The tires skidded and squealed, pulling the car into the other lane.

A horn blared as a pickup truck swerved around him.

Heart thundering, Alex pulled his car off to the side of the road and struggled to catch his breath. He was shaking too hard to drive.

He knew better than to hit the brakes, but it had been instinct. Then he'd nearly been hit by an oncoming truck. He could've gotten himself killed, then he'd never see Zoey again.

Alex took a deep breath. "Stay focused. This is all about Zoey."

He sat up straight, ready to get moving again.

The dog stood about ten feet in front of the car, its ears and tail perked up.

"Move!"

It didn't.

Alex punched the horn.

The dog sat, not taking its gaze from the car.

What was he supposed to do now? The dog wasn't giving him enough room to pull back into traffic.

It barked, staying in place.

"What, are you Lassie? Want to lead me to Timmy?"

The dog barked again.

"I don't have time for this!" Alex hit the horn again.

It didn't move.

Of course it didn't. Alex wasn't going to get out of the car. Not after what had happened last time.

"Move!" He pushed the horn, letting it run for a full twenty seconds.

The dog stayed put and barked more.

What if the dog actually wanted Alex to follow it? Could its owner be hurt out there?

The police *were* taking care of Zoey and Ava. Maybe Alex could help someone else who was in need.

Unless it was a trap. He'd be stupid to walk into something like that again.

The dog rose to its feet and inched toward the woods, limping, and continuing to bark at Alex, but not giving him room to move the car.

Alex pulled out his phone and called Nick.

"What?" Nick answered. His voice was strained.

"What's going on?"

"They're negotiating with Dave. He's got Ava. That's all I know."

Alex swore. "I'm so sorry, Nick."

"They've got the best of the best there." Nick's voice wavered. "If anyone can get her from him, it's them."

"Is Zoey there?"

Silence.

"Nick?" Alex exclaimed.

"Dave claims he let her go days ago."

It felt like a punch to the gut. Dave wouldn't let her go. Captors didn't do that. Either she'd escaped, or... Alex couldn't let himself go there.

"There's a dog here, not letting me drive."

"What does that have to do with anything?"

"I think it wants me to follow it into the woods."

"Alex, stop and think."

"What if it found Zoey? I need to follow it, as crazy as it seems."

Nick took a deep breath. "Where are you? I'll call it in."

Alex glanced at the GPS and told Nick.

"I'll call it in. Stay in the car."

"I've got my conceal carry." Alex patted his gun.

"Alex..."

"Call it in, but if Zoey's out there, nothing's going to keep me from her."

"I know. Just be careful."

Alex ended the call and scrambled out of the car.

HELD

Ava fought back tears as the gun dug into her scalp. There were so many officers surrounding them, but her dad wasn't one of them.

Where was he? Going through the cabin behind them to take Dave by surprise? Or maybe she just couldn't see him. It wasn't like she had a great view.

Dave dug his nails into her arm and muttered, "Quit struggling."

Ava wanted to lash out, but she couldn't even speak much less fight back.

"Did you hear me?" He pressed the gun harder against her skull.

She gave a little nod just to get him to ease up.

Dave yanked her back, hurting her neck. "I'm going to shoot her if you all don't leave! Now!"

Nobody moved. Not a single gun pointed in their direction turned away.

Ava's breath caught. Were they that sure he wouldn't hurt her? Or did they think they could take him out before he killed her?

One man stepped a little closer. "Let Ava go, then we'll leave. We just want to bring her home safely to her family."

"Then you'll leave me alone?" Dave took sharp breaths and tightened his grip around Ava.

"Yes. Her family wants her home."

Dave's ragged breathing was loud next to her ear. Then he did the unthinkable. He pulled the gun away from her.

Ava's entire body went limp, and Dave almost lost his hold on her. He swore at her then, waved the gun around at the officers. "You must think I'm stupid, right? If I hand her over, you're not going to let me go! I watch documentaries. I know how this works. Either you'll drag me to jail or kill me."

"Dave, we just want everyone safe. That includes you."

"You don't care about me! I've got a gun to my stepdaughter's head!" He shoved the gun against Ava's temple.

She wanted to tell him she wasn't his stepdaughter, but with tape over her mouth, she wasn't saying a thing.

"Dave, we don't want to see anyone hurt. Not even you."

The man kept saying Dave's name. Was that some kind of technique to calm him? Or build trust between them?

"Liar! You're all liars! Nobody cares about me. No one ever has, especially not now. The whole world hates me."

"Dave, we want to help. I don't know what anyone else thinks, but I can see that everything you've done is a cry for help. Let me be the one to give that to you."

"No!" Dave readjusted his hold on Ava.

The gun clicked in her ear.

Her breath caught. Was he about to shoot, or had he only bumped something on the gun?

She was still alive and not hurt, so he hadn't shot. Not yet, anyway. It was probably only a matter of time.

"Dave, would it help if we all step back and give you a little space?"

"Just leave!"

"As soon as you hand over Ava, Dave."

"My only leverage? You'll shoot me! Never. I'm not dying here."

Stars danced before Ava's eyes. She was too scared and breathing shallow and quickly, not getting enough air. She closed her eyes and tried to block everything else out.

It didn't work. Ava focused on breathing, instead. She managed a couple deep breaths, and it seemed to help. She opened her eyes and kept her gaze low. There were so many people with guns aimed at her and Dave.

The one guy kept talking to Dave. He was obviously saying whatever he could think of, trying to get him to let her go. But Dave had nothing left to lose, even Ava knew that. He'd shot up a school and kidnapped two people. Once they arrested him, he would never get out.

That was almost a relief, except for the fact that he currently held a loaded gun to Ava's head. She'd watched him put the bullets in. He'd wanted her to see. To know what he could do if she didn't cooperate.

Ava tried to focus on what the negotiator was saying. Anything to get her mind off being seconds from death. All Dave had to do was to pull his finger, then it would be lights out for her.

More tears stung at the thought of it. Never seeing her family again. Her friends. Never telling Braylon how she felt and not knowing if he returned the feelings. Losing out on the chance to experience all her dreams. She needed to apologize to Parker for being a jerk to him the morning of the shooting.

She couldn't hold back the tears. They spilled onto her cheeks and ran down her face.

Why couldn't the cops work faster? Couldn't someone just jump Dave and knock the gun from him? It couldn't be *that* hard.

Except everyone was afraid that he would shoot her. With her being so young, they were probably extra careful. Or at least she hoped.

"Will you take an exchange?"

Ava tried to turn toward the feminine voice, but Dave had too tight of a hold on her. She moved her eyes as far as they would go.

Officer Foster stood off to the side, staring at Dave. "Take me instead."

Ava's eyes widened. What was Tinsley's mom doing?

"Just let Ava go. She's young and innocent. She doesn't deserve any of this. I'm a cop. Wouldn't you rather put a gun to my head?"

Dave shouted profanities at her and demanded she get out of the way.

"Let the girl go." Foster's voice was smooth as honey. "If you care at all for her or her mom, do this one thing. I'm willing to step in her place. You can still negotiate what you want."

One of the other officers ordered Foster to back away.

The negotiator also said something along those lines.

Ava could barely think. Her knees wobbled and threatened to give out.

Dave jammed the gun harder against her head and whispered for her to hold still.

Her bladder was about to give out. In front of all these people. More tears ran down her face.

"Take me," Foster stepped closer. "You can do whatever you want to me. We'll get you anything you demand. Just let Ava go."

"Get away!" Dave's finger moved slightly on the trigger.

The sound echoed louder than anything else in Ava's ears.

Pee flowed down her legs.

He swore and, for a moment, loosened his grip on her.

Ava flung her weight forward. The ground came at her faster than she could comprehend.

Shouting and gunfire sounded all around about the same time she hit the forest floor. Dirt flew into her eyes and she inhaled it up into her nose. Feet moved all around her, kicking more dust into the air.

Someone or something tugged on the ropes around her back.

"I'm trying to help. Hold still, honey." It was Foster.

Ava closed her eyes. Relief ran through her, but also fear. What was going to happen next? Could Dave still shoot her? Or had they taken him down?

"It's going to be okay." Foster pulled loose one of the ropes.

Ava wanted to scramble to her feet, but her body wouldn't cooperate. It was like her muscles had all given out at once.

More ropes came loose. Ava's arms fell to the sides. Then her legs rolled away from each other.

"This might sting." Foster ripped the tape from Ava's mouth.

She spit out the gag and struggled to breathe.

Foster helped her to sit. "I need you to walk. Can you do that?"

Ava nodded, though she wasn't sure her body would cooperate.

Foster put her hands under Ava's arms. Ava took a deep breath and forced herself to stand. She shook but managed to take a step. Then another until they reached the end of the cabin.

Ava turned to look at Dave. She needed to know if he had been restrained or killed. Either way, he had it coming.

He had cuffs on his wrists, behind his back. One cop was shouting at him while another read him his rights.

"Are you okay?" Foster asked.

Ava turned back to her. She shook her head. "I thought I was going to die." Her voice cracked and tears spilled again.

"Oh, honey." Foster pulled her into an embrace and squeezed.

Ava relaxed a little in her arms. "Where's my dad?"

"He'll meet you at the hospital."

"He's not here?"

Foster rubbed her back. "He wanted to be, but it wasn't possible. Come on. Let's get you to the ambulance."

Ava stepped back and met her gaze. "Were you really going to take my place? As Dave's hostage? Or was that just something you guys say?"

"I meant it." She nodded. "I wasn't supposed to do that, but I had to step in. I'll probably be put on desk duty for a while for that, but it was worth it."

Ava threw her arms around her.

CHASE

Alex ducked under branches and jumped over exposed roots as he followed the dog, who could take paths he couldn't. It moved around stealthily despite its limp.

He kept his eyes and ears alert for danger, though he trusted the canine far more than he trusted people. At least if he was headed for a trap, he had his weapon ready. He would shoot without hesitation.

The dog slowed, sniffing the ground. Alex used his phone as a flashlight to see what had caught the dog's attention.

Blood.

His heart skipped a beat. It wasn't Zoey's, was it?

It could be anyone's. There was no reason to think it belonged to Zoey. What were the chances that the dog jumped out in front of Alex's car?

It was probably someone else's blood. The dog's owner, that's what made more sense. Zoey didn't have a pet.

Alex took a deep breath. "Come on."

The dog glanced up at him and twitched an ear. Then it crept forward, keeping its nose close to the ground.

Alex's heart raced. Hopefully he could help the owner quickly, then get back to his car to meet Zoey at the hospital. The cops *would* find her. Alive. They had to.

The dog slowed again.

Branches rustled nearby.

Alex froze. He kept one hand on his gun and the other on his phone. He shone the flashlight around.

Sniffling sounded on the other side of a bush. The dog walked around, then looked at Alex.

"Hello?" He shone the light from side to side.

"Is someone there?" The voice was weak. Scraggly.

Familiar.

Alex's heart jumped into his throat. He raced around the bush.

Zoey lay in a ball, her eyes red and bruises and dried blood covering her. Her shirt was ripped and bloody.

It took a moment for realization to settle. She was actually there in front of him. Alive.

Alex flung himself on the ground and pulled her close. A million thoughts and emotions ran through him, making it impossible to talk.

"Alex?" she whispered.

"It's me." The pain in her eyes gutted him. He kissed her hair over and over.

"How'd you find me?"

"How could I not?"

She pulled back and ran her palms across his too-long beard. "Am I dreaming again?"

"No, baby. I'm really here. Let's get you to the hospital." He clung to her, resting his head against hers so she wouldn't see his tears.

"But Ava—"

"The cops are already there." His voice wobbled. "It's you they couldn't find. Come on." Though he urged her, he couldn't get himself to move.

She pulled back again, then wiped a tear away. "I'm so sorry..." Her voice trailed away.

"You have nothing to be sorry for." Alex pressed his lips on hers and kissed her deeply. Zoey didn't return the kiss. He needed to get her to the hospital, but he never wanted to let her go again. She was right there, she was safe. And he didn't have to confess any wrongdoing to her.

She pulled back, her expression unreadable. "You taste like alcohol."

Except that. He had to confess to drinking. Alex nodded. "I'm sorry. I couldn't handle you being gone. The thought of—" His voice cracked. He cleared his throat. "It was too much for me."

She scooted back and kept her gaze averted. "Now you have to start over with your sobriety."

"How can you be worried about me?" He shook his head in disbelief. "Let's get you to my car."

She grimaced. "I don't think I can walk. Everything hurts."

"I'll carry you, then." He tucked his arm underneath her legs and rose to his feet, somehow keeping his balance. His heart was racing and his legs were unsteady, but he managed.

Zoey leaned her head against his. "I can't believe you found me. He left me there to die."

Fury surged through Alex. He fought to keep his voice steady and soft. "Never doubt my love for you."

"I don't."

Alex stumbled along, trying to recall the path he'd taken in. At one point, he had turned right.

The dog trotted in front of him despite its limp, took the path to the left, and gave a small bark.

"This way?"

It limped on ahead. Alex followed, clinging to Zoey. He never wanted to let go. Yet he would have to at the hospital.

Her breathing grew deeper, more rhythmic. She was sleeping.

She probably hadn't gotten any decent rest since she'd been taken. Alex understood that all too well.

He pushed through some bushes and came to the road, just a few feet from his car. An ambulance and two police cars surrounded it, lights flashing. Someone was tending to the dog's broken leg.

"Zoey, wake up."

"Mmm..."

"The medics are going to fix your leg and check out your other injuries."

She opened her eyes and held his gaze. "Don't leave me."

"Never."

HOSPITAL

Nick's legs nearly gave out as he pulled back the privacy curtain and stared at his baby girl lying in the hospital bed with tubes attached to her.

Ava's eyes lit up. "Daddy!"

He ran over and wrapped his arms around her, falling to his knees. "You're okay. You're really okay."

"I am now. They wouldn't let you help find me?"

"Not officially. But I was the one who figured out where Dave's cabin was."

"You were? How?"

Nick closed his eyes. As much as he'd love to throw Corrine under the bus, he couldn't do that to Ava. "It doesn't matter. The only thing that matters is that you're safe."

"And Dave's going to jail."

"He won't get out, either. Not after what he did. You don't have to worry about that."

"Where's Mom?"

Nick grimaced. "She's at the station, honey."

"Is she in trouble?"

He needed to tread carefully with his words. "She's answering some questions about Dave."

"Because they were together?"

Nick nodded, still unable to meet her eyes.

"Do they know about Mason?"

"What do you know about him?" Nick sat on the edge of her bed and squeezed her hand.

Ava grimaced. "The creeper is my half-brother."

Nick wanted to demand how long she'd known and why she hadn't told anyone, but he already knew the answer—Corrine would have told her to stay quiet. Instead of speaking, he just nodded. "None of them can hurt you."

"Anymore."

Nick took a deep breath. "Right. Anymore."

"Daddy, I'm tired."

He leaned over and kissed her forehead. "I'll let you get some sleep."

"Are you going home?"

"I'll stay here. If I get tired, I'll sleep in that chair." He nodded to the seat next to the bed.

"Thanks." She gave him half a smile, then closed her eyes.

Nick didn't budge. He couldn't stop looking at her. She was safe and sound. The nightmare was over.

Although there was still plenty to deal with, such as making things right with Foster. If she would talk to him after the whole towel incident. And him ignoring her after fleeing her apartment.

He'd be lucky if she ever spoke to him again. If she was mad enough, she could file a report on him.

He had been so stupid to give into his desires like he had.

Regardless, he would have to face the consequences, whatever they may be. Hopefully she would give him some grace considering the circumstances.

If not... At least Ava was home, safe and sound. He could always get another job if it came down to that.

Nick wandered out of the room, lost in thought.

Anderson stood outside the door. "Hey, boss."

Nick gave him a slight nod. "Detective."

"I'm glad Ava's safe."

"Thanks."

"Does this mean you'll be back to work?"

Nick leaned against the wall. "Give me a few days."

"Understood. Did you hear about Foster?"

"What about her?" Nick tried to keep the worry off his face.

"She's the one who saved Ava."

"She is?" Nick exclaimed.

"Well, it was a team effort, but she offered herself in place of Ava."

Nick closed his eyes and took in the news.

"She's on paid leave for breaking protocol, but I can't see that lasting. Especially not since she saved the hostage."

Genevieve had risked her job and her life to save Ava, even after everything Nick had put her through, whether intentional or a misunderstanding.

"You okay, Captain?"

Nick opened his eyes and nodded. "It's been a rough patch. I'm just glad it's over."

Anderson nodded. "I don't know about you, but I could use a really boring year at the office. Maybe two years."

"That's something I could get behind. Hey, do you know where Gene—Foster is? I'd like to thank her."

"I know they wanted to look her over, but I'm not sure if she's here at the hospital or if she was checked out at the site and let go."

"It's okay. I'll find her."

"If I hear anything, want me to let you know?"

"Yeah, thanks." Nick headed down the hall, where some blue uniforms were gathered, talking.

He questioned them, but none had seen Foster since back in the woods.

Nick went to the waiting room and texted her, asking if she was okay.

She didn't respond.

He tried not to take it personally. She might be driving or filling out paperwork or answering questions about the incident. Or she might never want to see Nick again. And he couldn't blame her.

The thought of not seeing her again, or of having a cold businesslike relationship, hurt worse than he wanted to admit.

Now that Ava was safe, and especially since Genevieve had been the one to free her from Dave, Nick's feelings for the officer nearly suffocated him. He wanted to hold her in his arms and thank her with kisses and gifts.

If she would let him.

RESTING

Alex pulled into a parking spot in front of his apartment building and glanced over at Zoey, who was still sleeping. She'd fallen asleep before they'd left the hospital parking lot two hours earlier.

"Zoey," he whispered.

She didn't even flinch. Poor thing was probably tired enough to sleep for days.

Alex climbed out and went around to her side, opening the door carefully since she was half leaning on it. He unbuckled her, scooped her up, and carried her to his apartment.

Once inside, he was glad she was asleep. He'd really made a mess of things while she'd been away. That would have to wait.

Alex brought her into the bedroom, pulled the covers back and laid her down. He pulled off the shoes someone had given her back at the hospital, then tucked the blankets around her and kissed her lips lightly.

He stared at her, still hardly able to believe that she was actually there with him. She was even more beautiful than before.

A warmth radiated through him. He wanted to protect her from any more harm, and he wanted to be the best husband he could be. Their wedding date couldn't come fast enough. Maybe they could move it closer.

She mumbled something and rolled over. He fixed the covers, then wandered around the room, picking things up. Then he went through the entire apartment, gathering the bottles from his drunken stupor.

He took them down to the recycle bins, glad to be rid of the evidence even though Zoey already knew about him giving into the drink.

Back inside, he picked up all the other messes scattered about. He'd really been living like a pig.

Alex didn't want Zoey seeing any of it, so he used up all his nervous energy making the apartment look nice. It still didn't hold a candle to how well Zoey kept hers, but at least it was better. The only thing he couldn't fix was the mirror that now looked more like a spider web, thanks to his fist.

At least he hadn't cheated on Zoey. He'd only blacked out, then wallowed in his misery missing her.

Alex leaned against the wall and slid to the floor, still staring at the mirror. His gut churned as he thought about how close he'd come to losing everything that mattered to him. He didn't know what he would've done if he'd lost Zoey, either to death or his own stupidity.

He raked his fingers through his hair and yanked.

"Don't ever do anything that stupid again, Mercer!" He jumped up and glared at himself in the uneven mirror. One eye was higher than the other, but that didn't stop him from giving himself the most furious look he could muster.

Once he was convinced he'd gotten through to himself, he wandered around the apartment again, picking up a few more stray items.

That reminded him of the horrible morning he'd found Zoey's clothes. If he was going to stay sober, he needed to start going to the meetings. Marking the days on the calendar wasn't enough.

And now that Zoey was back, he needed to make sure he didn't fall of the wagon again.

Finally, the exhaustion set in. He trudged back into the bathroom, threw off his sweaty clothes, and took the longest shower of his life. He fought to keep his eyelids open as he pulled on some shorts and shirt, then climbed into bed and wrapped his arms around his fiancée. With her there, he fell into a deep sleep.

When he woke, light streamed in from the windows. Zoey was thrashing around, twisted in blankets, muttering something he couldn't understand.

Alex brushed some hair away from her face and spoke softly. "Zoey, it's okay. You're safe now. I'm not going to let anything happen to you."

She struck him on the chest, then her eyes flew open. They were wild for a moment until recognition settled. "Alex."

He pulled her close and held onto her tightly. "I'm here. I'm not leaving your side for anything."

Zoey went limp and broke down sobbing.

Alex's heart shattered worse than the bathroom mirror. Tears stung his eyes, then ran down his face into Zoey's hair.

"It was horrible. A nightmare I couldn't wake from." She gasped for air and sniffled. "I really thought I was going to die. But I just kept on fighting."

He rubbed her back. "I know, baby. I know."

She clung to him and told him everything from the moment Dave showed up at the school office until Alex found her in the woods.

He cried along with her through the whole heartbreaking story. "It kills me that I wasn't there."

Zoey pulled back and stared into his eyes. "Maybe we should take Ariana and move as far away from this place as we can."

Alex arched a brow.

"This whole town is cursed, don't you think? It's practically the abduction capital of the world. Let's leave it behind and start over."

He took a deep breath. It was easier said than done, especially since Zoey's parents were Ariana's legal parents, but he didn't want to shoot down her idea. "We can talk about it."

She frowned. "You think it's a stupid idea?"

Alex shook his head and ran his fingers across her cheek. "Not at all. I just think we need to give it some time and think everything through, that's all."

"What's there to think about?"

He traced her lips, letting his thumb linger. "At least meet Caden Alexander first."

"Who?"

"Our nephew."

Zoey's eyes widened and she sat up. "Macy had her baby?"

"I almost had to deliver him."

"What?"

Alex sat up, held her hand, and explained what happened.

Zoey closed her eyes. "I was supposed to be there. Does she know why I wasn't there?" Her eyes flew open. "You didn't tell her, did you? She doesn't need that kind of stress!"

"I didn't tell her. I'm not sure if Luke did, though. You were gone a long time, and you know Macy. If she wants to know something, she won't stop until she gets answers."

Zoey flew out of the bed. "We need to tell her I'm okay. What about Ariana? Does she know what's going on?"

Alex shook his head. "She's been down with the flu. Nobody told her anything."

"Thank God. I never thought I'd be so happy about her being sick." Zoey grabbed her overnight bag from the floor. "I'm going to take a shower, then we're heading over to see everyone. I need to give everyone big hugs."

"Yes, ma'am. Is your ankle okay? Can I help you?" He scrambled out of bed.

"It's fine. I only twisted it, remember what the doctor said? I barely feel it now. Fix your hair, okay?"

"Whatever you say." He wrapped his arms around her. "Just know that everything will be fine. We're together, and we'll face everything side by side. You couldn't get rid of me if you wanted."

She relaxed a little and her mouth even curved into a tiny smile.

Alex pulled her closer and pressed his mouth to hers. He held onto the taste of her, the feel of her, everything. Now that she was back, he was determined to appreciate every moment. Every small detail.

OVER

Nick paced his condo. He needed to get back to work. The kids were all in school—Parker and Ava had been bused to two different neighboring middle schools—and it had been days since Dave's and Corrine's arrests.

Despite his disdain for his ex-wife, Nick had tried to get her out of jail for the sake of the kids. But letters found in her garage had proven she'd been more involved with Dave's sick plot than first thought.

She and Dave had planned on running away together with all three kids and then returning to the East coast for Mason where he was staying with his grandmother. Corrine already had fake identification for all of them. The shooting and bomb had been nothing other than a distraction for the authorities while they made their escape. She had stayed with Parker after discovering she couldn't get to Hanna because of the elementary school lockdown.

Then she was waiting for Dave to kill Zoey before bringing Parker and Hanna to the cabin, but by that time she had decided she preferred Nick to Dave, so she was going to stay and leave Ava with Dave until she could sneak away to get her.

The woman could rot in jail for all Nick cared. And she would. Neither she nor Dave were going anywhere.

He still hadn't heard anything from Genevieve. Neither Parker nor Ava had seen Tinsley at their temporary schools.

The pile of paperwork that was sure to be sitting on his desk would get his mind off everything. At least until it was time to pick up the kids. Then he would need to plaster on his smile again and pretend everything was okay. It wasn't, and they knew it, but someone had to be positive.

Nick ran a comb through his hair and headed for his Mustang. His mind wandered as he drove. The kids were begging him to move them all into Corrine's house.

They did have a point—the condo was cramped with all four of them. He and Parker in one bedroom with the girls in the other. The house had all the things he'd lost in the divorce. Nick would just have to get rid of Corrine's things. Much of it had already been taken in as evidence. Half the job would be over.

He only needed to be able to buy it. It wasn't like Corrine could afford it in prison, and between selling his condo and not having three child support payments, he would easily be able to make the mortgage.

It was a possibility, but he didn't want to let the kids know that unless he could actually make it happen.

Once in the parking lot, Nick texted a friend who was in real estate. Then he headed inside.

Everyone greeted him with wide smiles, congratulations, and high-fives. It warmed his heart that everyone was so happy for him about Ava being brought home safely.

His joy melted away as soon as Chang stepped out from the bathroom. Their gazes locked, and the haughty officer's face paled.

Good.

Nick lumbered toward the other man.

Chang cleared his throat. "Welcome back, Captain."

Nick gritted his teeth. "My office. Now."

"Right."

They walked in silence to Nick's office—he'd been right about the stack of papers. Nick closed the door behind them and drew the blinds.

Chang swallowed but stood tall.

"Have a seat."

He sat.

Nick waited a moment before he took his seat on the other side of the desk. Then he pressed his palms on the desk and stared Chang down for a moment before speaking. "You need to understand something."

Chang nodded.

"You are an officer. I'm the captain. You don't blackmail me. Try it again, and you'll not only lose your job but you'll never get hired anywhere else, either."

"I—"

"I'm not done. You're going to be the best-behaved officer on the force. Got it?"

Chang arched an eyebrow.

"Does the Oasis nightclub mean anything to you?"

His face paled and he looked like he was going to be sick. "How did you...? I mean, there's no evidence—"

"Oh, but there is. And I found it. I *have* it."

Chang glanced around the office, breathing heavily.

Nick leaned over his desk. "It's not here, and it isn't at my home or anywhere else you might think to look. It's safe. But one wrong move, and it won't be. It could get into the wrong hands. All too easily."

Chang clutched the sides of the chair, his eyes wide and face continuing to pale. "I could lose everything."

"I know." Nick let that settle for a few moments. "Do we have an understanding?"

"Yes, sir."

"Now, I'm sure that whole thing was a misunderstanding. Maybe you were framed. Who am I to say? You're a good officer, other than your head being too big. You going to keep that in check?"

Chang nodded.

"Good. Get out of here."

The other man jumped from his chair and fled the room, leaving the door wide open.

Nick got up to close it but watched as Chang raced to the bathroom. At least that was one loose end he didn't have to worry about any longer. All Nick would have to do would be to say "Oasis" and Chang would shape up.

He went over to his desk and flipped through the tall stack of papers. Oh, the glorious life of a police captain. He separated the pages into four different piles, but couldn't bring himself to start going through any of it just yet.

Nick wandered over to the door and glanced out at the cubicles. Many were full, but one in particular was empty.

A little too empty.

He wandered over to Genevieve's desk. All personal items had been removed. This was more than an administrative leave.

His heart dropped. She'd left the force. That was the only explanation.

Nick yanked open a drawer, hoping it was a mistake. Maybe someone had put the photos of her family and Tinsley in there.

Just office supplies. He went through all of them, finding nothing of Genevieve's.

Hardly able to breathe, he stumbled back to his office and locked the door. He crashed onto the couch and fought to catch his breath.

She'd left without so much as a text.

He'd messed everything up. They'd had such a good thing going. Now it was over before it had even had a chance to start.

Maybe he could try and find her to at least talk about what had happened.

SECRETS

Z oey wiped some mist from the mirror and studied herself in the small space. Almost all the bruises were gone, though the rope burns around her wrists were still there if she looked hard enough.

Her ankle had been back to normal pretty much since she returned from the hospital. But that had been the least of her concerns.

She had a couple small scars—nothing that wouldn't heal.

It was the internal wounds that worried her. The nightmares hadn't stopped. One after another, every single night.

She'd kept everything to herself after giving all the details to the doctors and police.

Alex had asked so many questions. He only cared, of course. The love and devotion in his eyes was undeniable.

That was what made it worse. She couldn't bear to tell him *everything* that had happened. She'd left out the worst assault. She could hardly handle thinking about it.

But at some point, she was going to have to tell him.

Zoey studied her now-clearer reflection, her gaze landing on her stomach. She rested her palm over her belly button.

Her period hadn't shown in the time she'd been back. She kept telling herself it was from the stress.

But deep down, she knew the truth.

She was carrying a psychopath's child. And it was also hers.

Yes, she would have to tell Alex about Dave's final assault on her. There was no getting around it.

Tears welled in her eyes. She turned away from her reflection and pulled on her clothes.

Hot, angry tears spilled onto her cheeks. She'd thought she'd gotten them all out in the shower.

Zoey took a deep breath. It was time to put on a happy face for everyone. She and Alex were taking Ariana to hang out with Nick and his kids.

As she applied her makeup and fixed her hair, she thought about things that made her happy. Her daughter's beautiful face. The love of her fiancé. Little baby Caden Alexander.

Zoey gave herself a quick once-over. She looked normal, despite barely hanging on inside. She stepped into the hall and smiled at Sparky—named by Ariana—then patted him between the ears. "Almost time to get that cast off your leg, huh?"

The faithful dog leaned against Zoey's leg, wanting her to pet him some more. She obliged, partly wishing she could just stay in her apartment with him for the day. But she knew that every time she got out and lived her life, she not only grew stronger but she also gave Dave a figurative kick in the groin.

She would win, not him. Her whole life was in front of her. He would be behind bars for the rest of his days if there was any justice in the world.

Ding-dong!

Sparky ran over to the door as best he could, barking happily.

Zoey took a deep breath and hurried over to open the door.

Alex stood there, holding a bouquet of colorful flowers. He held them out for her. "These made me think of you."

She took them from him, then wrapped her arms around him,

squeezing as tightly as she could as she blinked back tears. "You're perfect, you know that?"

He snickered. "Hardly, but I'm glad you think so."

"You are." Zoey held him for a few more seconds before stepping into the apartment and putting the flowers in a vase. She kept her back to him so he wouldn't see her struggling to keep her emotions in check. All she wanted to do was run to her room and give in to the tears. Instead she turned to Alex and smiled widely. "You're a dream come true, you know that?"

He came over and pulled her close. She stiffened at his touch, but quickly relaxed.

Alex frowned, obviously aware of her initial reaction.

Zoey raked her fingers through his hair. "Thank you so much for the flowers. I'm going to take pictures and show them off online."

He traced her lips with his thumb. "Are you sure you're okay?"

She kissed his thumb. "Of course. What makes you ask?"

"I just can't help but think there was more to your ordeal than you're letting on."

Zoey swallowed. It was so hard to keep anything from him. Alex had literally known her for his entire life. But she wanted to live in this fantasy of everything being perfect for as long as she could.

"You and your overactive imagination." She threw him a forced teasing glance. "Let's pick up Ariana before she starts to think we aren't coming."

Alex cupped her chin. "You know you can tell me anything, right? Nothing can change the way I feel about you, Zo. Nothing."

She spun around, unable to look him in the eye. "I know."

Zoey talked about some work drama as they headed to the car with Sparky in tow. She didn't let Alex get a word in edgewise until they reached her parents' house to pick up Ariana, who proceeded to talk nonstop about the play she was trying out for. Zoey relaxed as Alex's attention moved to their daughter.

Once they arrived at Nick's house, all thoughts of Zoey's problems faded into the background. The house was full. There were a handful of neighbor kids crowded around the dining room table, playing a game and laughing.

Ariana raced to join them. Ava glanced up from the game and met Zoey's gaze, then smiled at her. Zoey relaxed. At least Ava had managed to bounce back—she even held the hand of a cute boy with wavy hair falling in his eyes.

Alex took her hand and squeezed, giving her a smile that could still melt her insides, despite everything she'd been through.

Maybe Zoey could bounce back one day, too.

AUTHOR'S NOTE

Thanks so much for reading *Against All Odds*. I've been wanting to write a book with a school shooting for a while now. Not because I want to take advantage of a popular topic, but because I often work through issues by writing them out into a fictional story. Hopefully reading provides a similar experience for you, as well.

I did my best to handle the subject matter with care. I find it incredibly disheartening that this happens. The worst I ever experienced in school were kids pulling the fire alarm and the occasional fake bomb threat. We had one lockdown drill when I was a senior in high school. Now kindergarteners have those drills. It's just sad. This sort of thing should be the furthest thing from the mind of any child.

My thoughts and prayers are with all the victims of shootings and their families and friends.

Anyway, if you enjoyed this book, please consider leaving a review wherever you purchased it. Not only will your review help me to better understand what you like—so I can give you more of it!—but it will also help other readers find my work. Reviews can be short—just share your honest thoughts. That's it.

Thank you for your support! I really appreciate it—and you guys!

NO RETURN

If you enjoy the Alex Mercer thrillers, you will like *No Return*, a standalone related to the series. Rusty is a friend of Alex's mom, and when he looks into his estranged sister's suicide, he discovers something far more sinister afoot...

~

Rusty reached for the doorbell, but stopped when he heard a commotion across the street. He backed up and glanced down a couple houses. A lady stood with her arms folded, staring at two other ladies storming off.

He went to the sidewalk. "Is everything okay?"

The lady turned to him and shook her head. "Never cross the Calloways."

Rusty tilted his head. "Who?"

She threw her arms in the air. "Be glad you don't know." She climbed into a car and sped off, peeling the tires.

"Okay..." Rusty went back to his sister's door.

Yelling sounded from inside. It sounded like his brother-in-law. Rusty recognized his voice from the phone. His stomach twisted in knots. Maybe this trip was a bad idea. He rang the doorbell, anyway.

"Coming," called Chris, sounding far less angry than a moment earlier.

The door opened, and a man with short, dark hair and dark eyes answered. He had a five o'clock shadow and dark circles underneath his deep brown eyes. "Rusty?"

He nodded and held out his hand.

Chris shook it. "Come on in. The police want me to come back down to the station. Do you mind staying with the kids?"

"That's why I'm here."

"You're a lifesaver. This last week has been a nightmare." Chris turned around and led Rusty up the stairs. He went left, and gestured toward a gray sectional couch with stuffing coming out of the armrests.

A girl, about thirteen, with hair as dark as his sat with her eyes closed, dancing in her seat to music only she could hear in the earbuds. A boy, about eleven, with light brown hair hanging over his ears had his full attention on the television. They both had the same dark bands under their eyes as their dad—the very ones Rusty was so familiar with, too.

"That's Kaylie. And that's Brady."

Neither glanced up.

"Kids!"

Kaylie pulled her earbuds out and Brady paused the show. They both turned to Chris, their eyes bloodshot.

"This is your Uncle Rusty. He's going to watch you guys while I'm out."

"I don't need a babysitter," Kaylie said.

"Me, neither," Brady said.

"I'm not here to babysit," Rusty assured them. "Just here in case you need something. Lunch, maybe?"

"Grilled cheese," Brady said and turned his show back on.

"I apologize for their manners." Chris turned to them. "Kids, be nice."

"Yeah, yeah." Kaylie stuck her earbuds back in and closed her eyes.

"Sorry to run," Chris said. "But make yourself at home. Thanks again."

"No problem." Rusty set his suitcase next to the couch on the brown shag carpet.

Chris hurried down the stairs, and neither kid seemed to notice. He stopped near the front door and his phone sounded. Chris's face clouded over as he glanced at the screen. He swore about a text.

"Is everything all right?" Rusty asked.

"What?" Chris looked at him, his face noticeably paler.

"Are you okay?"

"It's the CEO of my work. He's... I need to get the cops off my back so I can get back to work."

"Doesn't your boss understand you've lost your wife? You need time to recover and—"

"The only thing Travis Calloway cares about is the bottom line."

Calloway? Wasn't that the same name the neighbor had said outside?

Chris cracked his knuckles. "What I wouldn't give for just one drink."

"You don't want to do that. You've been clean for years, haven't you?"

His expression pinched. "Yes, I'm the one who helped Mandy get clean. I'm not going to drink. I just want one sometimes, you know? If my idiot boss and the cops would get a clue, I'd be fine."

Rusty leaned against the cracked banister. "Surely, your boss can understand the need to—"

Chris's phone rang. He swore and answered it. "I'm doing the best I can, Ricardo. The cops have it out for me. They won't leave me alone." He paused. "I can't tell the police to wait! You're going to have to tell Travis I'll work nights or something. My wife just died."

Rusty turned toward the kids and watched them, trying not to eavesdrop on Chris.

"Look, Ricardo, I can't afford to lose this job, but I can't tell the cops to take a hike, either. They want me down at the station now. The longer you keep me on the phone, the longer it's going to be until I can get back to work... You can't do that me! I have vacation days." Chris let loose a string of profanities and put his phone away.

Rusty turned back to him. "Can I help with anything?"

Chris stared at him, his face reddening. "I hate that pompous jerk." He picked up a potted flower and threw it against the wall. It shattered, sending soil in all directions.

WHEN TOMORROW STARTS WITHOUT ME

If you enjoy suspense *and* romance, you won't be able to put this one down. Just read the preview and see what you think...

~

The railroad tracks rumble beneath my pink sneakers, vibrating my entire body along with them. My heart thunders in my chest.

I'm not backing out.

Sunshine beats down on me. It's early summer, but it's already proving to be an especially hot one. A rarity for a suburb of Seattle. It's too bad I won't be here to enjoy it.

Off to the side, near the shade of the trees, movement distracts me. Something is nearby. I can't tell what.

And I don't care.

The rumble of the tracks grows stronger. It's harder to balance.

My pulse races as the deep-throated horn blares through the air.

Though the driver clearly sees me, the green and yellow machine doesn't appear to slow.

Good. That's exactly what I want.

The horn wails again, this time rippling through me.

My right foot slips from the track. I land in the middle of the two long pieces of metal. It's probably for the best. I'll be hit by the center of the train. More force to end it all faster.

Squeal! Tssh...

The brakes.

No!

Don't stop!

Trains take forever to stop. Like half a mile or something. This can still happen.

I do the only thing I can. I burst into a run toward the massive, now-slowing vehicle.

The horn blares again, but I barely notice it. I can't let the train stop before it reaches me. If I'm going to get anything right in my life, it has to be this.

Now that I'm running, it's coming toward me faster. My heart pounds harder.

This is it. It's really going to happen. I can almost count down, but it would be too disappointing to get to zero, only to find out that I'd miscalculated.

The horn now sounds like a constant noise. That driver really wants me off the tracks.

He doesn't know who he's dealing with.

I'm ready for this.

Something hits me. From the side.

Wait, what?

Now everything is a blur. I'm sailing through the air sideways. Away from the train! It's leaving my line of sight.

My shoulder hits the ground first. Then my hip and side. My head hits. Hard.

I roll. Dirt and gravel get in my face.

I'm a mess of soil and grass.

The train barrels past.

I missed my train!

"What were you thinking?" demands a male voice from behind.

I spin toward the voice and glare at its owner. The gorgeous face of the owner. His almost-shoulder-length wavy hair is mostly covered by a gray beanie which perfectly matches his plaid flannel shirt.

"What were you thinking?" he repeats.

I jump up and dust rocks and grass from my jeans and shirt. "Me? What about you? Why'd you do that?"

He stands, but doesn't dust himself off. "You mean why did I save your life?"

"Yeah." I glower at him. My heart continues racing, but now from anger instead of excitement. "I had it all planned perfectly. Then you show up. The one variable I didn't take into account. Jerk."

He shakes his head. "You're unbelievable. I save your life, and you call me names."

"I called you a jerk. That's one name. Learn to count."

"Why'd you do it?" He adjusts his hat and tilts his head. His eyes are filled more with concern than annoyance now.

The guy is flipping gorgeous, but in the most down-to-earth way imaginable.

It's infuriating.

"What's so awful that a pretty girl like you wants to end it all?"

Pretty? Me? The guy obviously needs glasses. Maybe they flew off when he ruined my plans.

"Don't you have anything to say?"

"Not to you." I fold my arms.

"Hey, I saved your life. The least you could do is tell me why you were going to throw it all away."

I sigh as dramatically as I can. Seriously, I really draw it out and even manage a slight eye roll. Maybe I should've gone into acting. Too late for that. For anything, really.

There will be another train.

I ignore the hottie and storm toward the tracks. "This time I'm going to get it right."

He jumps between me and the tracks. "And if I don't let you?"

"You're going to try to stop me again?"

"Yeah." He knits his brows together, clearly daring me to try and stop him.

Why does he have to be so attractive? It's aggravating.

I clench my fists. "I've fought off guys bigger than you."

He arches a brow. "Really?"

"You'd better believe it. Wanna try me?" I step closer, ready to kick him where the sun doesn't shine for messing up my plans. I should be all over those tracks, yet here I am just arguing with a mysterious guy who shows up out of nowhere.

He steps back with a little laugh. "Okay, I believe you. Hey, why don't we grab something to eat?"

I just stare at him. He can't be for real. "You want to get some lunch? After this?"

"I'm hungry. Aren't you?"

"Doesn't matter. I didn't bring any money." I need to get rid of him so I can catch the next train. It'll be another fifteen minutes. Yes, I checked. Just in case something went wrong. I'm prepared.

He shrugs. "I have money. Come on."

It takes me a moment to realize what he said. "Now you want to pay for my meal?"

"Yeah. Come on."

"What? Am I your charity case for the day?"

He doesn't move a muscle.

My stomach growls. Loudly.

He chuckles and rubs the light dusting of facial hair across his cheeks. "Sounds like you could use something to eat."

"What I need is the next train!"

Why did I admit that to him?

"Let's get something to eat. You don't even have to tell me why you're out here. Just eat the food, and sit there being furious at me for saving your life. Sound like a plan?"

I clench my jaw, not wanting to give into him. My stomach rumbles again. Why did he have to bring up food?

"Well?" The corners of his perfect mouth twitch. He finds me amusing.

"Fine." I may as well get a meal for my trouble.

There will be other trains. And looking at this guy won't be the worst way to spend my last hour.

STORY WORLDS BY STACY CLAFLIN

Stacy is a *USA Today* bestselling author who writes about complex characters overcoming incredible odds. Whether it's her Gone saga of psychological thrillers, her various paranormal romance tales, or her contemporary sweet romances, Stacy's three-dimensional characters shine through bringing an experience readers don't soon forget.

If you haven't yet read the *Gone Trilogy* (the story of Macy's abduction as a teenager) then you should read that. You'll find out what happened and learn more about how Alex and Zoey grew close.

No Return and *Dean's List* are standalone spin-offs from that saga, featuring Rusty and Lydia. Rusty must prove his sister's suicide was actually a murder and Lydia must figure out if her husband is a serial killer.

If this is your first Alex Mercer thriller, then you definitely need to read *Girl in Trouble* (Ariana's abduction) and *Turn Back Time*.

OTHER BOOKS

If you enjoy reading outside the thriller genre, you may enjoy some of Stacy Claflin's other books, also. She's a *USA Today* bestselling author who writes about complex characters overcoming incredible odds. Whether it's her Gone saga of psychological thrillers, her various paranormal romance tales, or her romances, Stacy's three-dimensional characters shine through bringing an experience readers don't soon forget.

The Gone Saga

The Gone Trilogy: Gone, Held, Over

Dean's List

No Return

Alex Mercer Thrillers

Girl in Trouble

Turn Back Time

Little Lies

Against All Odds

Curse of the Moon

Lost Wolf

Chosen Wolf

Hunted Wolf

Broken Wolf

Cursed Wolf

Secret Jaguar

Valhalla's Curse

Renegade Valkyrie

Pursued Valkyrie

The Transformed Series

Main Series

Deception

Betrayal

Forgotten

Ascension

Duplicity

Sacrifice

Destroyed

Transcend

Entangled

Dauntless

Obscured

Partition

Standalones

Fallen

Silent Bite

Hidden Intentions

Saved by a Vampire

Sweet Desire

Short Story Collection

Tiny Bites

The Hunters

Seaside Surprises

Seaside Heartbeats

Seaside Dances

Seaside Kisses

Seaside Christmas

Bayside Wishes

Bayside Evenings

Bayside Promises

Bayside Destinies

Bayside Dreams

Standalones

When Tomorrow Starts Without Me

Sweet Dreams (Indigo Bay)

Sweet Reunion (Indigo Bay)

Haunted

Love's First Kiss

Fall into Romance

CPSIA information can be obtained
at www.ICGtesting.com
Printed in the USA
LVHW090818291119
638734LV00011B/1094/P